Never Again!

Historic Fiction telling the Human and Inhumane Story of the Tulsa Race Massacre of 1921 and Its Aftermath

D1253895

S U S A N   E .   A T K I N S

Fulton Books, Inc.
Meadville, PA

Published by Fulton Books 2021

ISBN 978-1-63710-666-2 (paperback)
ISBN 978-1-63710-667-9 (digital)

Printed in the United States of America

PRAISE FOR *NEVER AGAIN!*

Read Never Again! and you will hear, feel, and discover the deeply buried suffering, shame and secrets of the 1921 Tulsa Race Massacre, one hundred years ago. This story is the historical real thing, resonating with human pain and frustration all the way to today as the wrongs have not yet been made right. Perhaps the Centennial will instigate justice.

—Pat Atkinson, journalist and former
associate managing editor, *Tulsa World*

Horrifying history, inventive storytelling. Susan E. Atkins has taken the subject of Tulsa's shameful Race Massacre, grounded it in well-researched facts, and then lightened those brutal events with a novelist's eye for real life characters and surprising plot turns.

—Connie Cronley, Tulsa author and
citizen of the Cherokee Nation

A fascinating, well-researched but disturbing glimpse of American racial history. Susan E. Atkins' story takes the reader to the horrors of 1921 Tulsa, and the ensuing years of denial and injustice, with vivid imagery.

—Apple Gidley, author of *Fireburn*

Never Again! engagingly weaves together the past and present in this heartbreaking retelling of a tragic twenty-four hours in Tulsa that ended black lives and destroyed a thriving black community in 1921. The title is a statement, a question and a promise. A must read.

—Kim Hoover, author of *Girl Squad*
(2020 GCLS Awards finalist) and
current president,
Lambda Literary Board of Trustees

Atkins' timely and well-researched narrative may have more aptly been entitled *Not Again!* to the extent that it accurately captures the shadowy darkness of the human condition and the devastating consequences that emerge when hatred, inequities, lies, jealousy, and incitement catalyze in a devastating crescendo with shattering and irreversible consequences.

—Kimberly R. Mills, Ph.D., BCBA-D,
Senior Executive Director,
Virgin Islands University Center for Excellence in
Developmental Disabilities (VIUCEDD)

For nearly eighteen terrible hours, the madness of mobs blended with a toxic soup of racism, envy, and greed, then poured out in a genocidal flood of murder, arson, and looting to destroy America's thriving Black Wall Street. *Never Again!* is an exhaustively researched fictional account of the 1921 Tulsa Race Massacre that captures in gripping detail the horror of this deeply shameful incident, one largely erased from American history.

—Annise Parker,
Former Mayor of Houston, Texas,
and current Victory Fund CEO

Susan E. Atkins has done tremendous research to provide both a scholarly and anecdotal portrayal of what happened in Greenwood during the 1921 Tulsa Race Massacre. Her chilling reports of the events during the worse race massacre in American history should be read by all who seek to know the truth.

—Reverend Dr. Robert R. A. Turner,
Pastor of Vernon Chapel A.M.E. Church, Tulsa

Thank God for the grit of Black Tulsans.
                    —W. E. B. Du Bois, 1926

CONTENTS

PREFACE

I am often asked why I wrote *Never Again!* The history of the Tulsa Race Massacre is already well-documented in scholarly books and intensively researched articles. Why another? I grew up in Tulsa, Oklahoma, in the 1950s, 1960s, and 1970s. Like many Tulsans during those years, I never heard even a whisper about the horrors that took place there on May 31 and June 1, 1921. When I did learn of them, I became incensed and obsessed. I thought that what happened in the Greenwood District would make a fantastic play, and I still do, so I began to write.

I adore theater and thought this story lent itself to that medium. It might, but only in the hands of an able playwright, which—I discovered after two years, countless readings, and over seventy-five drafts—I am not. I left that project for dead.

Then in 2020, along came Black Lives Matter and ubiquitous cell phones recording the atrocities. It brought back the horrors of the Tulsa Massacre and the shame of my hometown, especially after Interstate 244, also called Martin Luther King Jr. Memorial Expressway, was the scene of a truck driver plowing through peaceful Black Lives Matter demonstrators in May of 2020. I could not leave it alone.

A good friend who is a published author suggested that since I had been writing prose all my adult life as a communications professional, I should turn my play into a book. She even gave me a brilliant outline for the arc of the story. I followed this invaluable guide from the start.

For those readers not inclined to tackle a four-hundred-page documentary, I have tried to write an accessible story in a way that is explicit about the inhumanity that took place in Greenwood in 1921. I hope readers find a way to connect with and perhaps feel a fraction of the pain and terror that must have gripped the hearts of the thousands of frightened—and many fearless—Black Americans protecting their homes, businesses, and families and fleeing for their lives. They were running from a marauding mob of drunk, armed white thugs—fellow Americans, fellow Tulsans. Although strictly segregated, Black Tulsans had no real cause to fear white Tulsa, until that day.

This is an important, albeit horrific, story about a Massacre that happened and then disappeared even though it had an enormous impact on generations of Black Tulsans and whites with a conscience.

*****

This country has a long, cruel history of the subjugation and destruction of African Americans, first brought here as slaves and considered subhuman and denied human rights in every conceivable way from then to now. Slaves laid every brick of what became Wall Street in New York and the White House in Washington D.C. America's rise to international wealth and leadership and most individual wealth were built upon the unpaid labor and oppression of African Americans, Native Americans, and immigrants, especially those who could not pass for white.

Never Again! is a story about how this historic dehumanization of African Americans manifested itself in one midwestern town in 1921. What happened in Tulsa was not an isolated incident. The summer of 1919 saw dozens of riots across the country in which Blacks were falsely accused or convicted of such serious infractions as crossing an imaginary No Coloreds swim line in the Great Lakes or looking at a white woman. Then, as now, the punishment for Blacks stepping out of their place was meted out by vigilantes and today's militia: frightened, angry white men. This hate and fear resulted in huge losses of life and property, primarily Black lives and property.

Until well into the first decade of the twenty-first century, the disaster in Greenwood was called the Tulsa Race Riot. Once real attention started being paid to the true horror through hearings and lawsuits extensively covered by news media, the name was changed and became more accurately called the Tulsa Race Massacre. Tulsa was by far the worst but neither the first nor the last such incident.

Digging in, I learned that soon after Emancipation, new Jim Crow laws were passed in the South and effectively, if not legally, enforced in the North and West. These laws ensured that the dominant white caste could continue to accumulate wealth at the expense of the subjugated Black class.

Then came peonage (binding laborers in servitude due to debt); redlining (declaring minority neighborhoods poor investment risks); the Great Society (creating a downward spiral of welfare dependency in minority communities); urban renewal (targeting the destruction of minority neighborhoods in the name of progress); and mass incarceration (uneven sentencing which has resulted in one-third of Black men and boys going to jail in their lifetime).

All of that was done deliberately to develop a permanent underclass and to ensure that Blacks in America would be an unending source of cheap labor.

Police forces were originally formed from patrols used to catch runaway slaves. This simple fact presaged police complicity in the Tulsa Race Massacre and perhaps the systemic racism so pervasive in our society and our police today.

It is easy to presume that the 1921 atrocities were covered up by whites to hide their heinous acts, a nod to their shame. However, I learned that Blacks were also reluctant to say anything because the perpetrators of the crimes were in the Blue and White—police and the Ku Klux Klan. Moreover, Blacks were afraid it might happen again if they brought it up.

Among the takeaways from this tragic saga—and I will paraphrase and add my own spin on statements made by Black activists, clergy, and educators—is this: We want future generations of Black children to know more about our country's Black history than slavery and the Civil Rights Movement. We want them to know that Blacks have been successful entrepreneurs, professionals, and educators as well as kick-ass athletes.

Amid the unrest today and unsettling intervention of federal force into local Black protests while avoiding confrontations with white protestors—like those who attacked the United States Capitol on January 6, 2021—we wonder and hope and pray: *Never Again*!

INTRODUCTION

Never Again! is about one of the most heinous atrocities to occur on American soil—in Tulsa, Oklahoma, on May 31 and June 1, 1921. Thousands of drunk, armed, and newly deputized white citizens invaded the thriving Greenwood District, murdered an estimated three hundred Blacks, tortured thousands more, destroyed countless lives, and incinerated nearly forty square blocks of successful businesses, professional offices, family homes, churches, and other institutions.

This work of historical fiction is the story of how this horrific tragedy was condoned by most Tulsa civic leaders and officials in 1921 and then hidden by them and later generations for seventy-five years. Even more, it is the story of Black Exceptionalism and Resilience, of the men and women who built Greenwood early in the twentieth century, an area Booker T. Washington, the noted educator, author, and adviser to presidents named the Negro Wall Street during a visit there a few years before. These men and women had become some of the wealthiest Black people in America, and in 1921, they lost it all in less than twenty-four hours.

*****

This story of the Tulsa Race Massacre is based on historical facts painstakingly researched by me and others for more than twenty-five years. While *Never Again!* is a work of fiction, it draws upon well-documented events and includes references to both real and fictional people.

The two central characters—Hattie Johnson Rogers and Lucy Ann Barnes—are fictional. Introduced in chapter 1, these characters were born within a year of the Massacre and live through the years of silence and the years of the struggle for reparations. They are best friends, soul sisters, and courageous fighters for justice. Their timeline extends from late 1921 through 2005, when the two elderly women remain disappointed about the lack of justice for victims of the Massacre and their descendants.

It should be noted that the backdrop for chapter 1 is the state's second-greatest disaster—the bombing of the Alfred P. Murrah Federal Building in Oklahoma City on April 19, 1995. My account of this heartbreaking event is drawn from multiple news sources covering the story. I reconstructed the movements and thoughts of first responder Chris Fields of Fire Station 5 based on those news reports. To protect the privacy of Aren Almon, whose one-year-old daughter, Baylee, became the face of children lost in the explosion, I invented Melissa Thurman to view the tragedy through another mother's eyes.

Introduced in chapter 2, Don Ross was a longtime member of the Oklahoma House of Representatives and a colorful and ardent civil rights activist for many decades. In several instances, I have made up words attributed to him, as Rep. Ross is crucial to the ongoing story of Greenwood. Obviously, he never spoke with Hattie and Lucy, as their characters are fictional.

Because I did not want to quote Rep. Ross in very many conversations he did not have, I invented legislative aide Wilbur McNeely and Atty. Charlie Crabtree for those conversations. Also, I put words in Rep. Ross's mouth that he did not speak at riot-related Commission hearings in chapter 13 and subsequent chapters. His quotes from the media are accurate, though not verbatim.

Three characters pivotal to the story—Dick Rowland, Sarah Page, and Dick's aunt Damie Rowland—are based on actual historical figures. By most accounts, Dick and Sarah sparked the Memorial Day conflagration by their interaction on an elevator in downtown Tulsa, as described in chapter 4.

For narrative purposes, I have taken poetic license with several facts related to these three characters. By most accounts, Aunt

Damie's real last name was Ford, but I changed it to Rowland for her name to match Dick's. In actuality, he was christened Jimmie Jones in Vinita, Oklahoma, but changed his first name to Dick and his last name to Rowland when he and Damie moved to Tulsa. Dick wore a diamond ring but not one in his front tooth; only the white press called him Diamond Dick. Football was not played at Booker T. Washington High School until two years after he left.

Most significantly, Dick was not killed in the late afternoon of June 1, 1921, as described in chapter 11. In fact, the sheriff secreted him to Kansas City during the upheaval. Sarah Page eventually went to Kansas City, but I do not know whether or not they got together. I have no knowledge of Damie ever going to Kansas City, and it is unlikely that she and Sarah were ever friendly. Dick died in the 1960s in a dock accident in Oregon.

Uncle Hiram Porter, another character introduced in chapter 4, deserves special mention. His name is fictitious, but the blind, double amputee veteran of World War I upon which the character is based was real. He sold pencils from his wheeled wooden platform and sang or whistled popular tunes for tips. He was brutally tortured to death during the Massacre.

Action in chapters 15 and 16, for the most part, takes place in Kansas City, Kansas. All secondary characters with important roles in those chapters are fictional. Jimmy Henderson, originally introduced in chapter 4, is conceptualized as a high school buddy of Dick Rowland. He helps Damie and Sarah escape Greenwood, then takes them to Kansas City. In my story, Dick arranges for them to live and work at the home of a white couple, Henry and Jean Adams, until the Depression drives them back to Tulsa in 1935. Since I have not been able to find out much about what life was like in Greenwood in the 1930s, I created a Depression landscape of my own design in chapters 17 and 18.

Many expressions and words I use in the book are painful to modern sensibilities. I used these expressions and words to reflect the mentality and popular use of the period. Likewise, I refer to the Five

Civilized Tribes who were driven to Oklahoma on the Trail of Tears. Today, they are more accurately called the Five Tribes.

*****

Almost every one of the barbaric acts described in the pivotal chapters 5, 6, 7, and 8 are documented in scholarly books and articles, many of which are listed in the bibliography. I have relied upon these and others of the dozens of books and hundreds of newspaper, magazine, internet, television, and radio articles, which have meticulously recounted both the horrific events of May 31 and June 1, 1921, and the subsequent cover-up.

To tell this story through the people most impacted by it and to make it readable, I condensed and combined backstories of many Greenwood founders and icons. I portray them as homegrown Tulsans, but most were not. In reality, these doctors, lawyers, and industrious entrepreneurs came to the Oklahoma and Indian territories to escape cruelty at home, to further their own fortunes, and to seek a better place for oppressed Black Americans to live in peace and prosperity—in short, to build a community of Black people for Black people.

Several of the doctors, lawyers, and industrious entrepreneurs featured in *Never Again!* are based on real-life leaders and builders of a thriving Greenwood. Ottawa W. Gurley, a wealthy Black landowner from Arkansas, and his wife, Emma, came to Indian Territory in the Oklahoma Land Rush of 1889. In 1906, they bought forty acres in North Tulsa to be sold "only to Colored." He formed an informal partnership with J. B. Stradford, and together, they developed the Greenwood concept. For a time, Gurley had been a sheriff's deputy for Tulsa, which led some in Greenwood to view him with suspicion. After the Massacre, he might have implicated other Black leaders to save himself, and he definitely negotiated to get Blacks to sell their property. He was not indicted and moved to Los Angeles after he lost everything in 1921.

J. B. Stradford was an Indiana lawyer and son of Kentucky slaves. He and his wife, Augusta, came to Tulsa in 1898 and bought vacant lots, which they sold to Blacks for development. He built the first and finest Black-owned hotel in Oklahoma—the Stradford Hotel—reputed to be as big and popular as any in Harlem. He was one of sixty-five Black men indicted for inciting the riot. Subsequently, he and his family left Tulsa and did not return.

My narrative imagines that Gurley and Stradford are sons of Indian slaves. Some, though not all, of the Indian tribes made freedmen—Blacks freed after the Civil War—tribal citizens and therefore entitled to tribal lands, and many worked the land together. In my story, the fathers of these two characters had gotten tribal land.

Dr. A. C. Jackson was born in Memphis in 1879, one of three children of former slaves. He attended the Meharry Medical College in Nashville, Tennessee, and practiced for a while in Tulsa and in Claremore, Oklahoma. After that, he trained with the Mayo brothers at the Mayo Clinic, and they proclaimed him to be the best Negro surgeon in America. Some of the surgical tools he developed are still in use today.

After training in Minnesota, Dr. Jackson returned with his wife, Julia, to Tulsa where he practiced medicine. He was shot and killed in the Massacre. I found no evidence that he had children but invented some to further tell Dr. Jackson's story. His suspected murderer, a teenager named James "Cowboy" Long, was arrested and charged with arson, not murder.

John and Loula Williams came to Greenwood in 1902 and built a garage, confectionary, several rooming houses, and the Dreamland Theater, the first Black entertainment center west of the Mississippi. They were among the wealthiest Blacks in America at the time of the Massacre. They quickly rebuilt the Dreamland Theater but were never able to fully recapture their fortune.

Andrew J. Smitherman was born in Childersburg, Alabama, in 1883, the second eldest of eleven children. His father owned a coal mining business, and his mother was a schoolteacher. He received his law degree from LaSalle Extension University in Chicago. As an attorney, he worked for William H. Twine, who owned the *Muskogee Cimeter* newspaper. He started the *Muskogee Star* in 1912 and, after moving to Tulsa with his wife, Ollie, and two children, started the

Tulsa Star in 1913. Smitherman and his family fled to the East Coast after the Massacre.

*****

White men and women, both real and fictional, play import-ant secondary roles in *Never Again!* Sheriff Willard McCullough and police chief John Gustafson were real people. Most of their actions cited in this story have been documented in historical accounts of the Massacre. However, I did invent conversations the two law officers likely would have had with key fictional characters and characters based on real people.

Richard Lloyd Jones of the *Tulsa Tribune* was real. His edito-rials are quoted mostly verbatim, but his looks and some personal activities recounted in this story are based on rumors. Tate Brady was a wealthy civic leader and prominent member of the KKK. He was active in fomenting the riot, probably for personal gain. Disparaged in later years, he lost his son and committed suicide.

Bobby Small, his no-account son, and his spoiled daughter are fictional, as is Bobby Junior's hapless friend Jasper Hicks. There really was a Real Estate Exchange that was gunning for the land in Greenwood. Merritt J. Glass was the head of the Exchange, and his actions were reported in the newspaper. Since I invented Bobby Small, his interactions with Sheriff McCullough and others are fiction.

When I began researching this story, I knew that not all whites were evil and not all Blacks were good, but the names of most white Samaritans have been lost to us. Maurice Willows, head of the Red Cross rescue effort, was real and a true hero. He worked tirelessly to protect Blacks not only from disease but also from efforts to steal their land and prohibit them from rebuilding their community. I invented Harry Whiteside, Gary Smith, and others helpful to Blacks to show some humanity on the white side of the equation.

By the beginning of the 1920s, one in every ten white Protestant men in Tulsa belonged to the KKK. Many were in positions of power and purportedly very involved in the Massacre. Where I could, I doc-umented this. Though I don't mention it in this story, the court-appointed attorney for Dick Rowland (who was never called to duty) was a founding member of the holding company for the Knights of the Ku Klux Klan, the Benevolent Association of Tulsa.

*****

It is difficult to believe that within a year of the Greenwood holocaust, more than eight hundred homes and businesses were rebuilt and Greenwood was back on its feet. This happened despite restrictive new ordinances and unwilling local suppliers. This well-documented, Phoenix-like rise from the ashes is mentioned in chapter 12 and fleshed out in the epilogue.

For the most part, the epilogue focuses on the lack of publicly funded reparations, memorials, and scholarships for victims of and descendants affected by the Tulsa Race Massacre of 1921. The epilogue ends with the hope that such a horrific, man-made disaster will happen *Never Again*!

CHAPTER 1

Oklahoma City

April 19, 1995

It is a typically stunning Oklahoma spring morning—glorious sunshine, crystal clear blue skies, warm breeze—not yet sluggish summer, bristling with potential. But Hattie is late. She had hoped to be first in line by this time at the Oklahoma District Office of the Social Security Administration in the Alfred P. Murrah Federal Building in Oklahoma City. She wants to iron out some paperwork in person.

A light-skinned African American in her early seventies, Hattie wears her salt-and-pepper hair pulled back in a bun. She used to be tall for a woman, five foot seven, but seems fairly average now and has probably shrunk a bit, she admits to herself. A big-boned woman with ample bosom and bottom, she carries a medium-brimmed straw hat. Though the sun is not beating down now, she knows it will by the time she gets out of the Social Security office, however long that may take.

A strong yet compassionate woman, Hattie Johnson Rogers retired just over ten years ago, after more than thirty years of teaching at Tulsa's only Black high school. That was also the year her mother died, and she winces at the thought of it. She misses her momma and still laments the many weeks and months of separation they endured during the Depression. "But Momma got to see me graduate with honors from Langston and get the job at Booker T. Washington High," she reminds herself. "Momma was so proud. Her scrimping and saving had paid off."

Hattie loved her high school kids. She was strict but kind and fair, and the students and their parents appreciated all of it. Thanks to her childhood memories of the Depression and the Dust Bowl, she knew what hard times were about and could empathize with children of single moms. She had been one herself, dirt-poor and barely managing to scrape by. Oh, things aren't as bad now, she admits, but during the early fifties, when she started teaching, there was still so much poverty in Tulsa's Black district, existing side by side with successful entrepreneurs and professionals in a booming, encapsulated economy.

Today, Hattie is modestly dressed in a simple pastel floral print shirtwaist with short sleeves, narrow collar, full skirt, and matching belt. She likes the popular animal print dresses but hasn't found her favorite animal yet. Her sensible flats are caramel colored, matching her purse. She still wears stockings. In spite of the heat and fashion, she cannot bring herself to go bare-legged, and she won't be caught dead in pants or the everything black in fashion these days. Hattie used to wear brighter colors when she was teaching knowing it brought more positive energy into the classroom. Now she doesn't like to draw attention to herself, though she is still quite a handsome woman at seventy-three years of age.

"Darn traffic. Getting over here was slower than molasses on a winter's day," she complains to herself. She loves to walk, especially in the cool mornings, and muses at how flat Oklahoma City is compared to the rolling hills of her Tulsa. It is almost 9:00 a.m. now, and even though she is on Fifth Street, she is over a mile from the Federal Building. Still muttering to herself, she says, "Could have saved time and gas money if I'd just put a stamp on it, but those Social Security folks can be pretty slack-jawed, and I'd like to start getting the proper amount in my check."

Hattie is stepping with care over some trash on the sidewalk that had fallen out of a large city trash can when it tumped over. Suddenly, all hell erupts, and the world turns upside down. A gigantic explosion throws up a towering mushroom cloud and sucks all the air from the street. A wave of destructive energy shoots across Oklahoma's capitol, nearly knocking Hattie off her feet. In that flashing instant of unimaginable apocalyptic impact and black smoke, a sudden tornado of dust and pink smoke barrels across the city, raining debris down on wreckage and confusion.

She instinctively turns away from the deafening boom and the screeching sound of the now billowing blizzard of black smoke. She doesn't know the cause of the giant explosion or how far away it is. All she knows is the terror shrieking in her head. The storm sounds like a runaway freight train. She runs half crazed back the three blocks to the car she borrowed from her best friend. She runs faster than she thought she could. The sounds of ambulance, police, and fire engine sirens are screaming closer now, and she is getting sicker as the smoke gets thicker.

Shielding her nose and mouth from the smoke with her straw hat, her eyes stinging, Hattie can barely breathe when she gets to the car. The smoke is so dense and dark she can hardly see her way through. Glad I couldn't park any closer, she thinks. The usual two-hour drive takes four times longer to navigate her way out of chaotic Oklahoma City and crawl back home to Tulsa.

*****

Calls go out to all first responders. Everyone in Fire Station 5 runs outside when they hear the blast. The smoke is so close they jump in their trucks and speed downtown. They stop on their way to help those injured, people who have fallen to the street due to the blast and debris. Chris Fields and the Station 5 team had other plans for today, some much-needed maintenance and cleanup around the station and the trucks, but now...

Later, news announcers would report that "the stench of alcohol from broken bottles fills some narrow alleys as if one of this neighborhood's well-known late-night parties had turned bad." But Firefighter Fields had a different take on the acrid aroma. There was an unnerving and overwhelming smell of nitrates, like you would smell at a shooting range.

*****

Turning on the car radio as soon as she can, Hattie flips through channels, at first hearing only maddening snippets like, "This is how we do it," but she quickly finds sobering news reports of the carnage. First on the scene is the local CBS affiliate.

"This is Robin Marsh, reporting from the Alfred P. Murrah Federal Building where an enormous explosion has blasted a crater into the ground below. A third of the building fell into that hole while every building around is turned to twisted metal. Cars parked near the building have been upended, crushed under chunks of the falling building, or are ablaze, driving more thick black smoke into the crystal-blue sky. Tremors are being felt for miles around."

Hattie can hear the crunching of broken glass in the background on the radio, and she still hears her heart pounding in her ears. The network building was ten miles away but began to shake immediately after the explosion, Marsh tells the audience, and all available reporters, helicopters, and cameras were quickly assigned to the scene.

"Office machines, desks, files, and furniture are strewn along these streets, which are covered with the guts of those offices. Elevators are dislocated from their shafts. On any given day, five hundred workers would be inside this federal building, built eighteen years ago in 1977. Today, this building, those workers, and dozens of children at America's Kids Day Care on the second floor are engulfed in flames and fear."

Throughout the day, radio and television announcers read the names of missing or wounded people. Numbers to call are read and posted along with emergency resource numbers. Hospitals are overwhelmed by the waves of injured. Hallways and parking lots become makeshift wards as the hospitals are inundated with the flood of human wreckage. And the news gets worse as Hattie's slog of a drive and the day wear on.

> In nearby apartment buildings, balconies have dropped to street level, where bars and restaurants are buried and chairs and tables turned upside down...

Civilians are being asked to stay away so that rescue workers can...

Emergency hotlines are being set up. To find out hospital information, please call...

The Alfred P. Murrah Building was home to the regional offices of several federal agencies, including the Drug Enforcement Administration, the Secret Service, and the Social Security Administration...

At this time, police have no idea what may have caused the explosion...

Hattie heard the helicopters overhead soon after the blast and now can hear them on the radio as the horrific news fills the airwaves—almost as acrid as the air outside. "Thank the Lord for air-conditioning," she tells herself, recognizing her thought as odd in the midst of such ghastly news.

"Is this another terrorist bombing?" a reporter asks an unidentified man on the street. "Could this be Middle Eastern terrorists, like the bombing of the World Trade Center two years ago?"

"I can't imagine terrorists targeting Oklahoma City," the man replies. "Oklahoma City is small by national standards, four hundred and fifty thousand God-fearing souls on the buckle of the Bible Belt. Most people assume it is a gas leak or some kind of accident."

Other reporters describe the horrible scenes.

Opened in 1977, the Alfred P. Murrah Federal Building was named for an Oklahoma native who became one of the youngest federal judges in US history, appointed by President Franklin D. Roosevelt in 1936. The FBI is investigating what or who may have caused this catastrophe.

From my vantage point, this area looks like a war zone. Ambulances, fire trucks, and first responders are rushing in and out of the area, and others are racing to Oklahoma City from all over the region.

Bodies are being pulled from the wreckage as first responders frantically search for survivors.

We have no idea how many survivors there may be. The death toll is rising by the hour.

Police are urgently asking us all to clear the area because they believe they've found another explosive device. This is the first we've heard that this was a bomb, and now another bomb threat.

*****

Melissa Thurman, mother of two preschoolers, had dropped them both at the Kids Day Care by 8:10 a.m. so she can get to her office a few miles away by 8:30. She is pulling into work at United Insurance Company when she hears and feels the explosion. Must be construction, she thinks. Always seems to be new construction somewhere downtown.

When she gets to her desk on the third floor, everyone is glued to their radios. A TV set is on in the break room. "Been an explosion at the Murrah Building," a colleague explains. "Must be a gas leak." Melissa is paralyzed. Robotically, she calls Kids Day Care, where she knows her friend Aren Almon should be dropping off her one-year-old daughter, Baylee. Fast busy. A number to call for more information is announced on the radio. She copies it and calls: "Please leave a message…" Another number is announced, and another and another, recorded messages on every one of them. "Dear God, please let them be okay," she prays, helpless and heartsick.

On the TV, one of the first responders, Chris Fields, is carrying a baby in his arms. When he reaches an ambulance, a paramedic tells him the vehicle is already full. There are people on the floor and on the ground waiting for a ride to the nearest hospital. The tall, muscled rescue worker gently places the dead baby on a clean blanket, kisses her, and briefly cries. Then he appears to gather himself and goes back to work, facing the horror, his grief, death, and the broken and bewildered survivors filled with fear and dread.

Melissa cannot breathe. The baby in his arms is Baylee. Melissa's body goes numb. She cannot feel her hands, arms, or feet. She stares blankly at the TV, hoping to will her friend's baby back to life. An enterprising photographer has snapped a photo of Fields crying and kissing the unnamed baby. To Melissa's horror, that photograph ricochets around the world and becomes the face of the children lost in the explosion.

Reports of the rescue efforts go on all day, and the number of survivors seems meager in comparison to the dead. It is not, but it seems that way. Hundreds are seriously injured, some blinded, several with heart attacks, many with broken bones. At least one woman has to have an arm amputated in order to be extracted from the debris.

Although police have repeatedly asked residents to stay away from the area, crowds gather as close to the carnage as they can. Collective moans rise each time another dead body is recovered, especially a child's body. Cheers sound as survivors are brought to ambulances or holding areas. Prayers are said aloud for those on gurneys, many with oxygen or plasma pumping into their bodies on the way to awaiting overloaded emergency vehicles.

*****

Hattie slowly navigates several hours of driving while fighting through nearly opaque smoke and stop-and-go traffic, first in the city and then on the Turner Turnpike. Sirens from rescue vehicles speeding to Oklahoma City punctuate her journey. Finally, she gets back to her home on Reservoir Hill, at the northern edge of Greenwood, Tulsa's oldest Black district.

She immediately runs to the television where her roommate and best friend, retired attorney Lucy Ann Barnes, has been watching and worrying almost all day. "Oh, thank God you're home! I was worried sick. Are you okay?" Lucy jumps out of her chair, rushing to hug Hattie.

"Oh, Lucy, I am so sorry I couldn't call. Traffic was hideous, and I just kept trudging back here. But what in tarnation is going on in Oke City?"

"Look at this helicopter footage, Hattie. The Alfred P. Murrah Federal Building was blown up this morning shortly after nine. It's a mass of tangled rubble. They think it may be Middle Eastern terrorists."

"That's what they said on the radio. I meant to be in that very same building by 9:00 a.m., but the good Lord and bad traffic saved me. Ironic that that building was the district office for the Bureau of Alcohol, Tobacco, Firearms and Explosives, isn't it?"

"News says may be over one hundred dead, perhaps twenty of them children. They say it is the worst act of terrorism in the history of the country."

"And that's a fact," Hattie exclaims.

"It is not," Lucy flatly states, her rimmed midnight-blue eyes flashing. Lucy and Hattie have been best friends since they met in high school. They were maids of honor in each other's weddings, baptized and raised their kids together, and buried their beloved mothers and husbands together.

"Well, isn't it the worst thing you've ever heard of?" Hattie asks.

"It is not!"

"All right. All right. Of course, I know what you're talking about, and I know what happened to our family, friends, the whole community, but that was seventy-five years ago."

"And there were maybe three times more people killed," Lucy says with a steely calm. "But they were Black people—Black men, women, and children—and nobody cared then or now about Black people dying. Aren't you sick to death that the only tragedies are those that happen to white people?"

CHAPTER 2

Worth the Fight

Spring 1997

On another sparkling spring morning, Hattie and Lucy are on their way to Oklahoma City to discuss the reparations and memorials proposed for the victims and families of the Murrah building bombing. "It's a long drive, Lucy, but not as long as my last trip, and I do always enjoy the ride in this beautiful car of yours."

"Guilt is a powerful motivator." Lucy chuckles. "At least RWD almost always sent me and Momma money, if nothing else."

"I love how you call your rich white daddy RWD."

Lucy was the love child of her Black mother, Violet, and a handsome, blue-eyed white veteran of World War I. Wealthy and married, he had met Lucy's mother at Oklahoma Agricultural and Mechanical College where she worked.

"Left me enough money in his will to buy this car and put something away for the kids and grandkids to go to college. I wonder what his widow thought of that. Harold and I had enough for our Elroy's Julius and Pearl to go to school, and now Julius and his wife are saving for their kids. RWD's money sure has made it a bit more comfortable for everyone." The opera-pop hit "Time to Say Goodbye" is playing low on the radio. "It's really something that Andrea Bocelli would team up with a classical pop star to make this wonderful music," Lucy says.

"Whenever I hear Bocelli's name, I think of that blind veteran friend of Aunt Damie's who was always whistling popular tunes," Hattie recalls.

They ride companionably in silence, Hattie thinking about how lucky the two of them have been. Lucy's rich white daddy sent her to Howard law school. Hattie's mother and her aunt Damie saved every penny earned from working for white folks before, during, and after the Depression to make sure Hattie got an education.

Very few Black women or men have enjoyed such blessings, and she and Lucy aim to do something about that. They want reparations for the victims of the 1921 Tulsa Massacre—compensation for the families, businesses, churches, and lives destroyed by rapacious white rioters more than seventy-five years ago.

They are meeting today with Oklahoma state representative Don Ross, the outspoken civil rights activist and journalist first elected to office in 1982. He had written a powerful op-ed piece published yesterday in *The Oklahoman* to remind folks that the so-called Tulsa Race Riot was an act of domestic violence resulting in more deaths and far more serious damage than the Oklahoma City bombing two years ago.

Though he can be outrageous and off-color, Hattie is so proud of Don, who had been her student at Booker T. Washington High School. She can't help herself. Don was always one of her favorites. Although not the brightest bulb in the pack, he had an endearing sparkle that remains to this day.

That morning, Hattie had chosen a burnt-orange shift dress she thinks may remind Don of his time at Washington High. The dress has a slightly full skirt, though not as full as in the fifties, with sleeves to the elbow and a high-scoop neck accented by her string of pearls. She also wears the matching Mabe pearl earrings her beloved Andrew had given her for their thirtieth anniversary. He bought them from Tiffany, she remembers—quite the extravagance. After each wearing, she lovingly places them in their cute little turquoise box in her bedside table.

*****

Lucy wears a no-nonsense navy-blue pinstriped pantsuit that compliments her white hair. Her cropped jacket, not the long style favored by taller women, has padded shoulders suitable to her slight build. Underneath, she wears a simple cream crepe blouse, a gold pendant hanging around her neck and earrings to match.

But Lucy isn't thinking about her looks. She's more concerned with the pros and cons of their case. Every time she thinks about it, she's incensed. How can reparations and a memorial already be underway for victims of the Oklahoma City bombing when nothing has been done seventy-five years after the nation's worst act of domestic terrorism? What she wants most of all are better educational opportunities for Black children. "One step at a time," she reminds herself.

As they approach downtown, Lucy thinks about the Black neighborhood not far from there called Deep Deuce where her mother delivered and raised her. Her momma used to talk about the Aldridge Theater, Slaughter's Hall, and other clubs, she remembers, where famous stars like Jelly Roll Morton and Duke Ellington played the same type of tunes she and Hattie are listening to on the radio today. Her mother, along with many Black women from Deep Deuce, had worked in the homes of white people until the Depression. But Lucy's not going to dwell on the Depression now. She and Hattie have more pressing business.

*****

Hattie admires the ease with which Lucy slips the sleek black Pontiac Grand Am into a parking space at the Oklahoma State Capitol on North Lincoln Boulevard. Inside, they take the elevator to the second floor, then walk the short distance to the suite of offices occupied by Rep. Don Ross and his legislative aides.

"Lucy Ann Barnes and Hattie..." Hattie starts telling the receptionist just as Rep. Ross rises from behind his large oak desk and steps through the open door. He looks very dapper in his flamboyant plaid jacket with wide lapels, no tie, and signature Chai necklace, the Jewish symbol for life.

"Welcome, beautiful ladies. We've been expecting you. Come right in. I hope the traffic wasn't too bad this morning. I'm so pleased to see you both. May I offer you some sweet tea, hard cider, or other refreshment?"

"Oh, we're fine, Don, er, Representative."

"Now you just call me Don, and I'll call you Miss Hattie if that's okay with you. I know I wasn't your best student, but I always respected your intellect and your compassion."

"Now don't you go flattering." The years have been kind to Don, Hattie thinks. Though in his early sixties and slightly portly, he has the vigor of a much younger man.

"I am so sorry to say I have to go to a goddamn committee meeting and then a shitstorm of a floor vote, which I also can't miss. So if you'll excuse me, I'm going to leave you in the capable hands of Wilbur McNeely, my top legislative aide, the dashing Washington Hornets fullback and another former student of yours." Steering them toward two chairs where they can sit, he bows and leaves quickly for his next meeting.

As they wait, Hattie remembers how Don hadn't known about the Tulsa riot until she brought it up in his Oklahoma history class. When she told the class about it, Don shot to his feet and exclaimed, "That can't be true," to which she replied, "Sit down and learn."

Not only did he sit down and learn but he also began a lifelong study of the riot, soon discovering that his grandfather Roy Jones had lost his grocery store that horrible day, something his parents had never told him, but he made sure to tell his children all about it.

Hattie was proud of all Don had accomplished. After graduating from Washington High in 1959, he spent four years in the US Air Force before returning home to work in a bakery, among other jobs. Soon, he became interested in journalism and started writing a weekly column in the local Black newspaper, the *Oklahoma Eagle*. In 1972, he left to become an editor at the *Gary Post-Tribune*. He returned in 1977 to be general manager of the *Eagle* and had remained in Tulsa ever since, distinguishing himself not only in journalism but also in community service, politics, and civil rights.

Don earned both a bachelor's and a master's degree from the University of Central Oklahoma, though it took him several years to finish. He was one of many Black students benefiting from two land-mark cases decided by the US Supreme Court during the fifties—*McLaurin v. Oklahoma State Regents for Higher Education* (1950) and the more famous *Brown v. Board of Education* (1954)—that disallowed the segregation of Black students in the Oklahoma state university system.

Wilbur McNeely interrupted her reverie by opening a door adjacent to the reception area. "It's a pleasure seeing you, Miss Hattie. I'm excited to be meeting with you and Attorney Barnes. Please come into my office."

Wilbur was three years behind Don at school and a popular football player. He still has a sturdy build, broad shoulders, and an even broader smile, which was always winning with the girls, she remembers. Slightly graying, he wears a soft-brown suit, light-blue shirt, and a fashionable striped tie with a smart Windsor knot. Though in his late fifties, Wilbur still has a youthful energy in his walk and words.

After the two women are seated comfortably in the legislative aide's office, Lucy speaks first. "Mr. McNeely, we're here to talk with you about the 1921 Race Riot," she says, mustering up her most lawyerly demeanor, which she hasn't used in a while.

"Of course you are. Did you see yesterday's *Oklahoman*? Representative Ross set them straight about what actually was the worst act of domestic terrorism in America, and it unfortunately was also right here in Oklahoma."

"Yes, I saw his editorial and am proud of him for writing it," Hattie interjects. "But now we need some action."

"And I'm sure we all agree it's well past time for some recognition and compensation to come to the survivors and descendants of the Greenwood riot, but it's going to be tricky."

"How so?" Lucy asks. "It seems pretty straightforward to me."

"I only wish it were. Not only are we talking about seventy-five-plus years ago. We're talking about white folks paying Black folks for something their ancestors did. And you know some of these crackers can be tighter 'n bark on a tree."

"And that's the God's own truth," Hattie agrees. "But you sound like you already have a plan."

"I never could pull anything over on you, Miss Hattie. This is a two-pronged attack. I presume you saw that the state of Florida gave reparations to the victims and heirs of the 1923 Rosewood Massacre a little while back."

"Saw that," Lucy says. "Wondered at the time if that could set a precedent."

"That's your fine Howard law training talking, and you are right. We've been doing some very preliminary work for Representative Ross to put together a team of excellent lawyers—a dream team, I should say. Charles Ogletree Jr. of Harvard and Johnnie Cochran Jr. of, well, you know his reputation."

"I know both of those gentlemen by reputation, Mr. McNeely. Very fine lawyers indeed. What chance do they give us?"

"It may be a little early for laying odds, Attorney Barnes, but Representative Ross's plan is to use this Oklahoma City tragedy and the recent Rosewood reparations as grounds for the Oklahoma Legislature to commission a study of the 1921 Race Riot," he says, using air quotes to indicate not exactly.

Lucy is beside herself with anger and explodes, "After only two years, white folks are raising a memorial about the bombing here— two years—and they are making reparations for the families of the victims. But after seventy-five years, not a thing has been done for the survivors and families of victims murdered and robbed and a community decimated by a white mob. It's not right."

"You might think that as a teacher, I'd welcome this idea, Wilbur," Hattie says, her voice bewildered. "But honestly, what good will a study do?"

"A fine question, Miss Hattie, and the answer is fairly simple. If we go straight to the courts or the legislature and ask for reparations, their first question will be, 'Reparations for what?' And then we likely wouldn't get very far. So the idea is to get a state-commissioned report that spells out exactly what happened, what was lost, and the extent of damages. That is precedent for reparations."

"That's probably a very good strategy," Lucy says approvingly. "You're not letting any grass grow under your feet. We could have saved ourselves a trip."

"Not so fast, Attorney Barnes. Representative Ross has instructed me to recruit you and Miss Hattie. You know everyone in Greenwood, especially the old-timers—meaning no offense—and you know them better than these fancy coastal lawyers. They will need a lot of help identifying and locating the witnesses and then getting them to agree to depositions. So before we initiate any legal proceedings, we need to get this study underway. Are you game?"

"You bet we are," Lucy answers for both herself and Hattie. "Sign us up. This is worth the fight."

CHAPTER 3

Black Wall Street—How and Why

Prior to Memorial Day 1921

Oklahoma has always been at the crossroads of Southern and Western culture where football is tantamount to religion. Oklahoma Territory was the end of the line for the Five Civilized Tribes (Choctaw, Chickasaw, Cherokee, Seminole, and Creek/Muscogee) and their Black slaves. Thousands were herded like cattle from their ancestral homelands, plush plantations in the Southeast, on the Trail of Tears between 1830 and 1850 by order of President Andrew Jackson. This was in spite of the fact that Black slaves who became soldiers in the War of 1812 were a significant factor in defeating the British.

> I expected much from you… But you surpass my hopes. I have found in you, united to these qualities, that noble enthusiasm which impels to great deeds.
>
> General Andrew Jackson,
> to the men of color at the
> Battle of New Orleans
> 1815

General Andrew Jackson to soldiers of color after victory in War of 1812

Land rushes in 1889 and 1893 brought more Blacks and white Southerners to the territory, and thanks to some of the biggest gushers ever discovered—Bartlesville, Red Fork, Glenpool, Cushing, El Dorado, and others—Oklahoma Territory became the largest oil-producing area in the country. Some of that oil, called Texas Tea, was on Indian land, resulting in some very wealthy Native American and African American men.

Approximately five hundred Blacks owned land in the territory, and by the time it became a state, Oklahoma had more all-Black towns than any other state in the country. Prior to statehood, Black activists of the day—led by former Kansas State Auditor Edward P. McCabe—tried to enter Oklahoma as the first Negro state in the union. That never got off the ground, succeeding only in angering the white majority.

Whites made their voices heard loud and clear. In fact, when Oklahoma became the forty-sixth state in 1907, Senate Bill 1, the first law passed by the Oklahoma Legislature, segregated waiting rooms in train depots. Throughout the railway system, segregated rail cars already were commonplace. Amenities in Colored cars ranged from sparse to nonexistent. The bathrooms were smaller, and there were no racks where Blacks could store their luggage, among many other inconveniences. Segregation was severe, complete, and strictly enforced in the new state of Oklahoma, perhaps nowhere more than in the city of Tulsa.

Tulsa (or Tulsey, as it was called in the early days) had never been much more than a cow town, a dust bunny at the intersection of Nowhere and In Between. But Texas Tea changed all that. Tulsa became the Oil Capital of the World at the beginning of the twentieth century.

By 1909, white Tulsa had paved streets filled with streetcar lines, cars, and bicycles, along with horses, wagons, and carriages. By 1920, nearly four hundred oil and gas companies were located in and around Tulsa. Many white men, though not all, were getting rich on oil. Thanks to Jim Crow, Blacks were forbidden to work in the oil fields.

SUSAN E. ATKINS

In addition to oil and football, war and patriotism were wor-shipped in Tulsa. Anti-Americanism was not tolerated. In 1917, a group of righteous Tulsa citizens in the Knights of Liberty abducted, beat, and poured hot tar and feathers on members of the Industrial Workers of the World. The vigilantes said the Wobblies were social-ists and therefore anti-American. In truth, they were prolabor, some-thing the oil companies could not tolerate. Tulsa considered itself the epitome of Americanism, but Americanism was a white-Protes-tants-only affair.

An almost total separation of the Black and white communities was achieved in Tulsa thanks to strict segregation enforced by law as well as geography. The Frisco tracks physically bisected the city between north and south—between Black and white. Most of white South Tulsa was clean and well-groomed and meant to stay that way, but west of Tulsa, across the Arkansas River, where oil refineries belched greasy, particle-filled black smoke into the putrid air, white working men and their families lived in squalor in Sand Springs.

Stench from the refineries permeated their one-room, ram-shackle shacks, dirtied clothes hanging on the line, and stuck to their grimy skin. Stench clung even to the meager meals prepared by the women—usually grits for breakfast, pieces of always stale bread for lunch (enough for the men, sometimes for the children, but rarely for the women), and some kind of potatoes for dinner.

Though a significant part of Black Wall Street was prosperous, most of Greenwood endured the same kind of conditions that poor, working whites had in Sand Springs, minus the refinery stink. Poor folks on both sides of the river had few, if any, sanitation facilities, almost no running water, and no garbage pickup, causing rats, cats, dogs, and hogs to fight for scraps in the streets. Many in both slums kept livestock in their yards and had outhouses built on stilts.

Like the poor whites, most Blacks, other than the privileged few, did not own cars in 1921. In Sand Springs, the public bus was decent, and a nickel-a-ride jitney service supplemented walking in Greenwood for the majority. Many wealthy Blacks had used their riches to build Tulsa's Black Wall Street, this alongside the wide-spread poverty. By 1921, Greenwood was one of the most affluent African American communities in the United States. For many Blacks, especially throughout the Southern United States, Tulsa must have sounded like the Promised Land.

At that time, the segregation forced on Greenwood might have worked more for Blacks than against them. Not bullied by whites, Blacks were able to run their own schools and businesses, and many entrepreneurs in North Tulsa were doing well in 1921. Economically mixed, Greenwood was self-contained, self-sufficient, and self-assured. Black consumers were doing business with Black merchants and professionals.

The Blacks who worked for whites in South Tulsa were also doing well. Waiters in white hotel restaurants could make a hundred dollars a day in tips. The maids, nannies, butlers, chauffeurs, and yardmen servicing wealthy white Tulsans brought their earnings back to spend in Greenwood.

Few, if any, white merchants would take the Blacks' money. Shopkeepers mocked and denigrated them, had them followed in their stores, and even searched them. Such iniquities made these proud African Americans want to see their own community, their Greenwood, prosper.

Black doctors, lawyers, teachers, and businessmen were prospering in their encapsulated economy, clearly defying the myth of Black laziness or incompetence. Much of the Greenwood District was bustling—home to twenty-four all-Black churches, a Black library, the Black Frissell Memorial Hospital, its own bank, and two Black newspapers, as well as hotels, restaurants, luxury jewelry and clothing stores, drugstores, grocery stores, nightclubs, garages, barbershops, beauty salons, billiard parlors, and a bus and taxi service.

Four theaters kept the area's residents entertained, including the Harlan movie theater and the very fine Williams Dreamland Theatre, the first all-Black entertainment center in Oklahoma. Live performances and silent movies accompanied by piano played in these theaters for Black patrons who did not have to enter through an alley or sit in the balcony.

Greenwood boasted the second-highest literacy rate in Oklahoma. Three-fourths of school-age children attended school, and Booker T. Washington High School taught Latin, chemistry, and physics. The proud community also had a Black trade union (Hod Carriers Local No. 199) and three all-Black fraternal lodges (Masonic, Knights of Pythias, and IOOF).

The best of the best lined both sides of Greenwood Avenue, the throbbing heart of the Black neighborhood. The better homes and professional offices were located on the east side of Detroit Avenue, which marked the western boundary of the area then referred to as Little Africa by the white press. Booker T. Washington had dubbed Greenwood the Negro Wall Street when he visited early in the twentieth century.

The seedier side of Greenwood was bustling as well—not rich but busy. Thanks to crooked police and corrupt public officials, lawlessness was the rule, not the exception, in Tulsa. Thanks to prohibition, moonshiners were doing a land-office business, and people knew Greenwood was the place to go to find most of them.

Rich white men drank at their private southside clubs or bootleggers delivered their illegal wares to white homes. Poor whites and Blacks mostly got what they wanted on the streets. By day, this was a rather smoothly functioning community with miscreants hidden in trash-filled alleyways. By night, home-brew hawkers, grubby gamblers, enterprising Black and white prostitutes, both male and female, and other denizens of the demimonde owned the streets. Many whites, not all of them poor, came to North Tulsa to enjoy the fleshy underbelly of the other side of the tracks.

Such was the Black Wall Street scene prior to May 31, 1921, the comparative wealth of a Black middle class side by side with Blacks living in squalor. The only common denominator was white Tulsa hatred for them all.

CHAPTER 4

Memorial Day

May 31, 1921

In the very patriotic town of Tulsa, the annual Memorial Day Parade is an enormous deal. At least it is an enormous deal for white veterans. This morning's parade had been no exception despite the heavy downpour. Dozens of motorcycle cops roared up Cincinnati Avenue followed by a few hundred white vets and a seventy-piece marching band. Several blocks away, Black veterans marched in uniform in front of a few jeering whites and hundreds of cheering Greenwood residents.

That afternoon, something happens that changes Black Wall Street forever.

*****

A blind, legless man comes flying down the Greenwood Avenue boardwalk on a wooden wagon. Suddenly, he tips over in front of Jones Grocery Store, tossing himself, his pencils, and his money cup into the muddy red dirt. "What on earth, Uncle Hiram?" says Damie Rowland as she uprights the wagon, lifts the legless man onto it, and starts picking up his pencils and money. "What happened here?"

A broad woman of medium height, Damie has milk chocolate skin. She is dressed in a pink-and-green plaid day dress with blue piping and a pointed collar, suitable for domestic service. Strong of mind, will, and body, she is smart but has no formal education. She even taught herself to play the piano because her church needed someone to accompany the choir.

"Well, I was just sittin' and whistlin' like I always does when some young boys come along and give my wagon a big shove I guess just to see what it do, and this is what it done." The offending boys are nowhere in sight.

Hiram Porter—Uncle Hiram to most—is a well-known fixture both in Greenwood and the white business district on the other side of the tracks. Wearing catcher's mitts to protect his hands as he pushes himself along the streets on his platform wagon, he scratches out a living by selling pencils and whistling popular tunes for tips.

Damie knows the brutality that has poured down on Hiram in buckets during and, especially, after the war. She knows he was blinded and his legs nearly blown off in France. His comrades would have left him for dead, except a big white feller carried him to the medics and told them to take care of the poor fellow, or they would have to answer to him. His legs were amputated with only whiskey for anesthesia, "and not much of that," he had told Damie.

After his surgeries, Hiram had been thrown onto a ship, probably in the galley since he could hear the rats scuttling nearby. Then he was tossed into the Colored section of a railcar like a sack of potatoes and finally dumped off at the Frisco station in Tulsa with no one to care for him. He told her once that soldiers who lost limbs while serving with the French got medals of honor, but he supposed that was only for white soldiers, at least if the US Army had anything to say about it. It hurts her heart to see him tormented now by local punks.

"What you doin' still off work? You off all day?"

"Well, Mr. Small came in this mornin' and said they're goin' to Muskogee after the parade to buy a new car. No warning, and just like that, I'm out a half day's pay. But at least it's turning into a pretty day, and I can clean my own house, maybe darn some socks for Dick." Damie had taken Dick Rowland in after his parents pretty much abandoned him when he was a child. "How is that boy o' yourn?"

"Oh, he's fine, Uncle Hiram, works all day, dances all night. Oh, to be that young agin. I'm gonna git me some groceries. You need anything?"

"No, thank ya kindly, but I be just fine," he says, whistling "Ole Man River" as he rolls away.

Damie goes inside and picks up a few things, including the Black-owned *Tulsa Star* and the white-owned *Tulsa Tribune*. Later, she reads a *Tribune* editorial that causes her a lot of worry: "While illegal drugs and alcohol are flowing out at County Line, our innocent white girls are dancing while these Nigger boys play the devil's own music. It's a disgrace and must stop."

*****

It is already brutally hot this steamy Tuesday afternoon, and sweat is glistening on Dick Rowland's blue-black skin. An ambitious nineteen-year-old, Dick is a tall drink of water, lean with broad shoulders. He has a diamond where his front right tooth would have been had it not gotten knocked out when he played football for the Washington Hornets in high school.

A flashy dresser, Dick wears a bright-yellow silk shirt with sleeves neatly folded up his shiny forearms. His pointy-toed coal-black cowboy boots are shiny too. He perfumes and powders himself every morning to keep the silk shirt from sticking. Luckily, he sweats more from his head and arms than he does from his torso, and he loves the shine of his silk shirts. "Hotter 'n hell, though," he admits to himself.

Aunt Damie brought Dick to Tulsa from Vinita twelve years ago when her brother and his mother split up, leaving him alone. A mean drunk, his father had knocked the hell out of him and his momma repeatedly, until one day, she ran out of the house, and he never saw her again. His only respite in Vinita was school, and he hadn't been so keen on that.

Things were better once he got to Dunbar Junior High in Tulsa, but memories of his sobbing mother, slobbering father, and rat-infested dump of a shack haunt him to this day. He tries not to think about it—much of that time is a blur in his mind—but he has vowed not to be the kind of man his father was.

Dick works hard as a shoeshine boy and is saving money to take him to Vaudeville. When friends gently remind him there are no real Black performers in Vaudeville, he tells them that the Chitlin' Circuit is better anyway. Reputedly one of the best dancers in Tulsa County, he cuts a mean rug out at the infamous County Line speak-easy with Black girls and white girls alike. He aims to do something with his God-given talent and good looks. He dreams of getting out of Oklahoma and building a better life.

*****

Hotelier Ottawa W. Gurley, better known as Andy, strolls down Greenwood Avenue with two lifelong friends—fellow hotelier J. B. Stradford and renowned surgeon Dr. A. C. Jackson. A rarity in Black Wall Street, all three men had grown up, married, and started successful businesses, including a prestigious medical practice, in Greenwood.

Andy Gurley is dark and stately. He and his companions are similarly dressed in conservative, well-tailored suits, starched white shirts with razor-sharp stand-up collars, and discreetly matching ties and handkerchiefs. All three wear fine Italian leather shoes, which they protect by carefully dodging the muddy puddles left by the morning rain.

"Remember when we were kids and ran up and down these streets like we owned the place?" Andy asks with a chuckle. "Well, now we do own the place—a good deal of it anyway. And despite many obstacles, we've established a strong community of Negro-owned businesses, churches, and offices of fine lawyers and brilliant doctors like Doctor J. here."

"Trained at the Mayo Clinic by William and Charles Mayo themselves and declared to be the finest Negro surgeon in the land," J. B. chimes in, proudly praising his friend.

Dr. A. C. Jackson is a short, bespectacled, light-skinned man with prematurely graying hair. His parents were poor. His father worked long hours in a clothing store, and his mother took in laundry to make ends meet. She also worked as a maid for two families in white Tulsa, commuting every day in time to be home when AC and his six brothers and sisters arrived from school. Neither of his parents was educated, but they knew the future Dr. J. was smart. They were determined to see that he got an education.

Andy and JB were more fortunate. Both of their fathers had been freedmen of the Creek tribe, meaning they had been freed from slavery after the Civil War. As a result, they had large land holdings—no oil but good farmland. Both boys preferred city life, so they went to school in Greenwood. They stayed with their respective aunties during the week but returned to help on the farm on weekends. Christened John the Baptist, JB was now the richest Black man in Tulsa. His recently completed Stradford Hotel, the first Black luxury hotel in Oklahoma, is where the Washington High School Junior-Senior Prom is to be held tonight.

"We've come a long way from our hardscrabble, red-dirt beginnings," JB reminds his friends. "But most of our businessmen are really shopkeepers. We need to think bigger. Even here in Greenwood, the white man owns a significant strip of the land where Negroes live or run small businesses. We should own more. Then we'll start getting some respect."

"With all due respect to you, JB, you're talking about respect from white folks, and I think that will take more than money," Andy declares. "But I tell you this: we could go a long way toward improving relations between the races in Tulsa if we could do something about the mixing going on out at the County Line.

"That opportunist Richard Lloyd Jones uses that yellow rag *Tribune* of his to fan the fires of fear and hate. He says the mixing of the races is an insult to the purity of white women. Any woman who frequents the County Line doesn't have much of a purity standard, if you ask me. And all the while the respectable, married Mr. Jones carries on with his secretary in his office in the Hotel Tulsa."

"Oh, he's a scoundrel, all right," JB agrees. "But really, I think he's just trying to sell newspapers. Of course, you know Augusta and I would never let our girls go out to a place like that, and no self-re-

specting Negroes allow their daughters to go to any speakeasies, especially the County Line."

After his two friends nod in agreement, JB continues. "But I will share with you my opinion, which you will likely abhor. We will never have peace until Negroes and whites mix up together completely."

"You cannot mean that," Dr. J. pipes in, aghast.

"I do most assuredly. Now I know that's not likely to happen anytime soon, what with the blatant discrimination visited on our boys in the Great War by their comrades in arms and all the torture and indignities heaped on our people before and after. But if we're ever to have peace, it's what must happen, gentlemen, total miscegenation."

"Well, I'd keep that opinion to myself if I were you," Andy warns. "In the meantime, those Real Estate Exchange boys are pressing hard to get all Negroes to sell our land and move out of Greenwood. They're hell-bent on a passenger depot and railhead for the Frisco railroad to build up a white commercial district and move our community farther out of town."

"And they get right ornery when someone tells them they can't have what they want, especially if that someone is a Negro," JB observes. "And do you remember that the KKK said a month or two ago that they are expanding membership in Oklahoma as if it isn't bad enough already? And now that fool Jones at the *Tribune* is printing editorials about how evil and sordid Greenwood is. Not a week goes by that he doesn't make some slanderous accusation about our community, usually on the front page."

"Unfortunately, there is some truth in what he says," Dr. J. replies to JB after a long pause. "We should do more to clean up our own backyard."

"True, but the white boys are now angry they ever allowed us to live on the wrong side of the tracks in the first place. They want that land, our land, and seem willing to do anything to get it."

*****

Dick crosses the tracks and walks into white Tulsa, toward the Drexel Building at Third and Main, the only building downtown with a bathroom that Blacks are allowed to use. Hanging back a couple of feet, he overhears two white men discussing the Greenwood situation.

Dick has his own opinions about the issue. He knows Greenwood is a gathering place for thugs and general evildoers, white as well as Black. He also knows that what the white man wants, he usually gets and by whatever means necessary.

He instantly recognizes the tall, barrel-chested man with ruddy, flushed skin and a bushy head of sandy hair—Bobby Small, president of the Real Estate Exchange, which controls zoning and licensing. His aunt Damie works at his house five days a week.

"Greenwood is nothing but a cesspool of whores and hooch, crooked games of chance and drugs, and a big black mark on the reputation of this fair city," Bobby grumbles. Having sent the family to Muskogee for a new car, he bellyaches with like-minded businessmen. "As the Oil Capital of the World, we have a chance to make Tulsey the finest city west of the Mississippi."

"Well, not as long as Niggertown is dragging us down. The Real Estate Exchange needs to do something, Bobby," complains his buddy Tate Brady, white civic leader, entrepreneur, and KKK member. "They call Tulsa the Magic City. Well, if we're so damn magic, why can't we make those Niggers disappear?"

"We're trying like crazy, Tate, but Niggers own most of Greenwood, and they're not interested in selling. Never should've let 'em buy any land at all. Something's gotta give."

Still thinking about the scary conversation he just overheard, Dick arrives at the shoeshine parlor at Second and Main. White customers pour in from the parade, their wet boots dripping with mud. "A quick shine, boy," says one.

"I gotta family picnic to git to," says another.

After hours of drying off and shining up dozens of boots, including his own, Dick finally has time to jive with Jimmy Henderson, his buddy since they dropped out of high school together to make money shining shoes. Dark-skinned, though not as dark as Dick,

Jimmy is dressed in Levi's, a denim work shirt, and his brand-new loafers just in from England. He's built like a linebacker—stocky but solid—even after quitting football two years ago. Dick knows his soft-spoken, thoughtful friend doesn't intend to shine shoes forever despite the good tips. Jimmy already works part-time at the Williams Garage, and if his boss is to be believed, he's pretty good at fixing cars.

"Did you see that *Tribune* article 'bout 'innocent white girls' dancing with Black boys whilst they play the devil's own music out at the County Line?" Jimmy asks, his dark eyes twinkling.

"I gotta laugh. Is they mad 'cause dem white boys cain't dance or 'cause dem white girls won't dance with white boys?" Dick giggles knowing both he and Jimmy have danced with some of those "innocent white girls" more than once.

Because Jimmy told him so, Dick knows their friends admire him for his good looks and style, his great dancing, and his amazing way with the ladies. He tries to keep his buddies laughing and usually succeeds. They also like that he brings Hiram Porter to the shoeshine parlor so he can sell a few more pencils and get him some of that oil-rich cracker coin.

"Hell, shoeshine's only a dime, but sometimes, dem punch-drunk honkies tip twenty-five cents or more. You'd git more money if you'd wear dat uniform," Dick has repeatedly counseled the World War I veteran. But every time, Uncle Hiram adamantly declares that he "ain't never gonna put it on agin."

It is late in the afternoon by now, and the sun is blazing. Saying he's got to pee, Dick heads off to the Drexel Building a block away. "Be careful," Jimmy calls after him. "Remember, this is white Tulsa we're in."

*****

As Dick boards the elevator to the Colored restroom on the second floor, he nods at the white operator, buxom seventeen-year-old Sarah Page. She is a pretty girl—not over five foot two with green eyes and a heart-shaped face framed by strawberry-blond curls. She ignores Dick and shuts the elevator door.

Sarah is full of life and loves a good time, though she doesn't show it at work. Her dark skirt stops just below the knee, showing off her shapely calves and her thin ankles. A tightly cinched waistband accentuates her waspishly thin waist. Her soft-cream blouse has gray trim on the pointed collar and cuffs and on panels on either side of the buttons below the modest V-neck. Still, her shapely figure is undeniable.

She doesn't dress so demurely when she goes out dancing, which she does most weekends and some weeknights. After a couple of drinks, she can be downright provocative, but she's all business on the elevator. It's her job to pilot the rickety old box up and down.

Sarah moved to Tulsa two years ago from Sand Springs. She says her parents died of the influenza, but in reality, she had a nasty divorce, which she never talks about. Leaving Sand Springs as soon as she could, she didn't tell her parents, uncle, brothers, or sisters where she had gone. She goes to secretarial school during the day and dreams of opening her own secretarial school at some point.

When the elevator returns to the first floor and the door opens several minutes later, Dick has his hands on Sarah's arms in a provocative position. He sees the looks on the faces of the white men waiting for the elevator, pushes the iron gate aside, and quickly runs out. Sarah appears to faint but doesn't fall to the floor. She simply slumps back onto her stool for a few moments.

Jasper Hicks, a skinny teenager in overalls, rushes to Sarah's side. He's kind of sweet on her and has tried to get her attention out at the County Line, though she never gives him the time of day. "Did that animal hurt you?" he snarls. As usual, Sarah ignores him.

A clerk runs over from Renberg's Department Store, also on the first floor of the Drexel Building. Together, he, Jasper, and some other men chase Dick down, tackle him, and drag him the four blocks to the county jail, scuffing his perfectly shined boots along the way, this in spite of Sarah's persistent cries that she's all right.

CHAPTER 5

Guilty before Charged

May 31, 1921 (Late Afternoon / Early Evening)

The sight of white men dragging a Black teenager through a thinning crowd of parade goers causes some to stop and gawk and others to sneer or even jeer at what they imagine must be going on. Almost before Jasper and the other men can get Dick to the county lockup several blocks away, newsboys are screaming, "Read all about it! Read all about it! Nigger arrested for attacking white girl in elevator! Read all about it!"

The newsboys work for the yellow rag recently purchased by Richard Lloyd Jones, who renamed the paper the *Tulsa Tribune*. Fast becoming infamous, Jones has been a white attack dog against Black Greenwood for months. Within hours, the *Tribune* published a front-page story headlined, "There's Going to be a Lynching Tonight!" Alongside, a previously written editorial demanding that city officials "kick out Negro pimps."

Once the men haul Dick into the Tulsa County Courthouse, Jasper tells the new sheriff that Rowland attacked Sarah Page, scratched her arms, and nearly tore off her dress. Sheriff Willard McCullough, a paunchy fifty-year-old with a walrus mustache, has lived in Oklahoma all his life and has heard his fill of stories about Black boys attacking white girls. He knows most of the accusations are trumped up, but he locks up Dick anyway.

The courthouse is located at Sixth and Boulder, just south of Cathedral Row, at the southern edge of the white business district and seven long blocks from where Greenwood starts at the Frisco tracks. The imposing, fortress-like structure with sweeping terraces and broad granite steps is typically surrounded by a city block of green grass, but recent rains have turned it to red mud.

Dick is taken by elevator up to the fourth floor, where the courthouse's three cells are located. The elevator and a single-file, narrow, winding staircase are the only access points. At the top of the stairway is a locked reinforced steel door. Sheriff McCullough turns off the elevator, stations three guards nearby, and tells them, "If anyone tries to get in, shoot to kill."

The news spreads like butter on a hot cinnamon bun in white and Black communities alike. Around 5:00 p.m., angry white men are gathering in front of the courthouse. "Give us the Nigger. Give us the Nigger," they chant below Dick's tiny fourth-floor window.

"Goddamn Nigger. What'd he think, he'd get away with it?"

"Attacking that poor, innocent Sarah."

"He's an animal."

"That diamond in his front tooth. Thinks he's slicker 'n snot on a doorknob, a real beast."

By 5:30 p.m., about thirty Black World War I veterans are assembled at the courthouse, most of them armed. Some are still in the uniforms they wore earlier that day in the Black Veterans Day parade. The vets offer to help protect Dick, to prevent the mob from lynching him, but Sheriff McCullough stubbornly declines their offer.

The whites are alarmed when they see Black men arriving with guns. Many rush home to retrieve pistols they put in their overalls or belts and rifles they brandish in their hands as they return to the scene. New extras spew forth from the *Tribune* extolling the virtues of Sarah Page, the innocent orphan from Sand Springs, who is working her way through secretarial school.

Additional front-page editorials call Diamond Dick a ruffian and a hoodlum who dropped out of high school and probably deals dope. These stories spread quickly through the white mob, further stoking their frenzy to lynch the prisoner.

It is a testament to the hate and fear of the white community that few question that a healthy young Black man would try to rape a white woman in broad daylight in the middle of the white business district in downtown Tulsa.

*****

Alone in his cell, Dick is scared and puzzled but not about to let his white guards get a whiff of his fear or doubt. "What the hell am I doin' here?" he wonders. "I didn't do nuthin' to Sarah, and she knows it. I don't think she tell it otherwise."

Dick recalls that seven months before, Roy Belton, a white boy accused of murdering a white taxi driver, was released to a similar mob from this very cell by the previous sheriff. The boy was lynched by that mob, and Dick has little reason to believe the same fate does not await him. "After all, I ain't even white!"

Yet Dick has a sliver of hope because of what he read in the Black-owned *Tulsa Star*, the only local paper to decry the Belton lynching. Sheriff McCullough, a career law enforcement officer, had to personally hang a young white boy a few years earlier in Pawnee. The boy was reading the Bible and asked the sheriff to give it to his momma after the hanging. He then told McCullough he was sorry he had to be the one to hang him, and Dick figured the sheriff was pretty sorry too. It was gut-churning to see the boy twitch uncontrollably once the rope snapped his neck, McCullough told the papers, and he hoped he would never have to see that again.

The three guards stationed outside Dick's cell are playing cards. "What kinda fool attacks a woman in broad daylight?" one of the guards asks with a smirk.

"Only a dumb Nigger," a second guard shouts in response.

"That's a lynch mob out there. I know it," Dick says to himself after overhearing the exchange. "What if they set the courthouse on fire? These boys ain't gonna help me none, that's for sure."

The fourth-floor cells at the courthouse are particularly ominous because there is a gallows at the end of the hallway. Just for fun, the third guard springs the loud trapdoor to let Dick know what likely will happen to him.

*****

Not long after 6:00 p.m., two men in white linen suits approach Sheriff McCullough, who is standing on the steps of the courthouse with a rifle in his hands and a pistol in his holster. He recognizes one as the very tall, very misnamed Bobby Small. He doesn't know the other sober-looking man, whom he assumes is from out of town.

"Good evening, Sheriff," Small says as he approaches the courthouse's steps. "We're here to take care of this unfortunate incident."

"Well now, that would be my job, gentlemen, and I thank you kindly, but I don't need your help."

"But, Sheriff, you know that Nigger is guilty as sin, and we intend to see that justice is carried out Tulsey style," Small pronounces, a large cigar jutting from between his fleshy lips.

McCullough knows Bobby Small came to Tulsa about a dozen years back to work for the National Bank of Tulsa. He impressed his superiors so much, so the story goes, that they elected him head of the Real Estate Exchange. According to gossip, he parlayed that promotion and the kickbacks he got through it to make a nice life in the prestigious Maple Ridge neighborhood for himself, his wife, his rotten son, and his spoiled daughter. Small enrolled both children in the prestigious new Holland Hall, an Episcopal private school. Bobby Junior was thrown out for drinking on campus, but Virginia is doing well and runs around with the right crowd.

"I'm right sorry to disappoint you, Bobby," McCullough responds. "But the law says that boy is entitled to a fair trial, and I aim to see he gits one."

"We don't need none of your legal shenanigan, Sheriff. Just turn him over and there won't be any trouble."

"You're right about that. There ain't gonna be no trouble. Anyone lookin' to go against the law here is gonna have to come through me, my deputies, and several loaded guns at the ready, so you boys just better clear on out. There ain't gonna be no show here tonight."

"Sheriff McCullough," the other man begins officiously, "you do not seem to be fully aware of the seriousness of the situation here. I represent a large national brotherhood. Many of your most respected civic leaders are members in good standing, I'm proud to say. And we have a great deal of experience in handling these matters."

The out-of-towner continues. "I'm not sure you understand that this is larger than your jail and larger than one sheriff in one town. Our brotherhood is dedicated to preserving the purity of the white race and honoring and protecting every white woman in this country. If we let these Niggers think they can go molesting a white woman in broad daylight, won't no white woman be safe anywhere in our great country."

"I have told you, mister, there will be no trouble here tonight," the sheriff responds. "And there will be no lynching. I will not release my prisoner to this here mob. I suggest you tell these men to go home. No one is comin' in or goin' out of my jail tonight."

Remaining near the courthouse steps, the two men confer and then make signals to others in the crowd. "Now you boys head on home," McCullough tells the growing white mob. "Dick Rowland is securely locked away, and there will be no lynching tonight."

But the crowd does not disperse, and the sheriff does not call on any of his sixty-four-man police force to help move the crowd along, nor does he stop the spokesman for the brotherhood from addressing the crowd. "The honor and purity of white women everywhere in America are at issue right here in Tulsa tonight. An orphaned young girl has been horribly violated. Will Tulsa stand for that?"

"No," the snarling crowd yells in return.

"Will Tulsa permit the savages to rule your fine city?"

"No."

"Will Tulsa stand idly by while officials abandon their duty to justice?"

"No."

"Will you ignore the safety of your wives and daughters?"

"No. No. No."

Despite McCullough's repeated pleas, the crowd does not disperse.

*****

Around 6:30 p.m., Dick looks down from his cell to see three well-respected Black leaders approaching the courthouse steps—A. J. Smitherman, editor and publisher of the *Tulsa Star*; noted surgeon Dr. A. C. Jackson; and J. B. Stradford, prominent Greenwood businessman. Despite noise from the crowd continuing to jack itself up, Dick can hear portions of the conversation.

"Good evening, Mr. Smitherman, Dr. Jackson, Mr. Stradford. To what do I owe this prestigious visit?" McCullough asks a bit sarcastically.

"We understand you have Dick Rowland under arrest in your jail, Sheriff," Smitherman says. "Is this true?"

"It is."

"Well, sir, this building is nearly surrounded by angry white men."

"And quite a few armed Black men," the sheriff retorts.

"This is true, Sheriff," Stradford agrees. "I believe some of our veterans have offered to help you protect the prisoner from this mob, but you turned them away."

"I told them and I'll tell you, JB, there will be no lynching tonight."

"With all due respect, Sheriff, this crowd is angry, and their numbers are growing."

"I done told you what I told them white boys: ain't gonna be no one hangin' from a tree in Tulsa tonight. The first man who tries to come through them doors will be lookin' down the barrel of my Smith & Wesson. Now, JB, why don't you see if you can quiet your people down. Just get 'em to calm down and go on home. Y'all have my word that boy Rowland will have his day in court. I guarantee you that."

The swelling mob grows louder and larger, drowning out whatever Dr. Jackson says to Sheriff McCullough. What Dick can hear makes him shiver: "Give us the Nigger. Give us the Nigger. Need to teach all them Niggers a lesson."

Earlier, Dick had overheard a bit of good news from one of the guards just outside his cell. According to the guard, white men attempting to break into the National Guard Armory "to even the arms race" were rebuffed by a "brilliant bluff" from the commander. Major James Bell told the would-be invaders that the armory was full of armed men there to protect state property, and the gang backed off. The guards laughed because they knew that no more than a handful of men were inside because the armory was rarely guarded.

In another slightly hopeful sign, Dick sees Walter White, a light-skinned Black man who easily mingles with whites, making his way through the crowd. Dick knows Walter will quickly report what he hears back to folks in Greenwood. Unfortunately, he suspects Walter will have to tell the folks that the white mob is angry and intent on lynching poor Dick Rowland.

CHAPTER 6

Rumble to Riot

May 31, 1921 (Evening)

At a hastily called meeting at the *Tulsa Star*, hotelier Ottawa Gurley reminds the Black veterans and others assembled there about the more than twenty-five riots that have taken place across America in the last two years. "Negroes never win those battles. The numbers are against us," he cautions.

"And I remind you of the over two hundred lynchings of Colored men during those same two years," a man in the crowd shouts. "So what do you expect us to do, stay in our place with hat in hand, stand by while another Negro man is lynched by a white mob?"

"We should take Dick Rowland outta that jail before them crackers storm the courthouse," yells Elroy Mann, a six-foot-four Black veteran.

Despite Gurley's urgent pleas to stay away from the courthouse or even leave town for the night, the veterans swiftly recruit reinforcements. By 7:30 p.m., they return to the scene to find that the mob has swelled to over two thousand white men, most of them now armed.

*****

The unruly white crowd, already loaded up on illegal moonshine, is riled up and feeling righteous, no doubt in part thanks to the constant drumroll of inflammatory editorials in the *Tulsa Tribune*. Just last week, an editorial written by Richard Lloyd Jones labeled Greenwood Niggertown, Little Africa, and a "cesspool of subhuman depravity" that must be cleaned up:

> A bad Nigger is about the lowest thing to walk on two feet. Give a bad Nigger his booze, his dope, and his gun and he thinks he can shoot up the world. And all these four things are to be found in Niggertown: booze, dope, bad Niggers, and guns.

Jones, a former cowboy and actor, is blond and handsome despite his bit of a potbelly. Although the son of a Unitarian preacher, he is as vicious as he is ambitious. A typically dapper dresser, tonight, he wears a vertical-striped shirt with bow tie, his dark pants held up by the suspenders he still prefers over the belts gaining in popularity. He paces and gesticulates wildly as his secretary takes dictation:

"The Oil Capital of the World, the cleanest and whitest city in the West, but we have a city drunk on oil, divided, and full of itself. Our city is a boiling pot. Lawlessness is rampant, and no one is safe from the stink rising up from the godforsaken plot of land that the Negroes are trying to claim as their own. But they are not properly maintaining the property of their white landlords or the Christian values of this fine city."

As he completes his diatribe, the married Jones roughly pushes his secretary onto the bed in the Hotel Tulsa room he uses as an office and raises her skirts above her head.

*****

"Git a rope. Bring us the Nigger." The chants in front of the courthouse grow louder. Around 7:45 p.m., Barney Cleaver comes out to talk to the Black vets assembled nearby. A graduate of Washington High, he is Tulsa's first Black police officer, a short man in his late twenties with caramel-colored skin. His beat is Greenwood, and he

58

has been told in no uncertain terms to make sure no Coloreds step out of line or cross the line.

Hoping to quiet the crowd, Cleaver tells the veterans not to pay any mind to the rabble-rousers. "Not all Tulsa whites believe us Blacks are guilty before charged," he says. "Dick Rowland is safe and seriously guarded. His cell is almost impossible to get to being high atop the courthouse."

"We know where that cell is," retorts a Black vet. "And a mob very similar to this one got Roy Belton out seven months ago and strung him up, and he was white."

"This sheriff does not intend to have a lynching on his watch," Cleaver replies. "That cell is as secure as that new Fort Knox in Kentucky. Sheriff McCullough won't be releasing Dick to anyone tonight."

The Black veterans are about to turn back when one of the armed white men suddenly tries to disarm Elroy Mann. "What you gonna do with that gun, Nigger?"

"I'm gonna use it if I have to," Mann yells in reply. A struggle ensues, a shot rings out, a white man falls dead, and all hell breaks loose.

*****

Ten whites and two Blacks are shot dead at the courthouse, a bare beginning of the untold misery to follow. Guns are blazing on both sides, and more bodies are dropping. A. J. Smitherman, father of five and publisher of *The Tulsa Star*, is one of the first to be shot and killed. Dr. A. C. Jackson and J. B. Stradford run for the safety of Greenwood, as do most Blacks in the crowd. Many are shot, wounded, or killed as they flee.

Beneath a billboard of Mary Pickford, America's sweetheart, an injured Black man is writhing on the street, bleeding from multiple gunshots in his abdomen and neck. When an ambulance and a white doctor try to reach him, the mob forces them back and starts hacking the dying man with their pocketknives.

Within thirty minutes, more than five hundred white men are deputized. Police officers haphazardly commission any angry white man who comes forward—sober or not—as a special deputy decked out with badge and ribbons. Each unarmed recruit is given a gun or told to go to a sporting goods or hardware store and get one. Soon, many deputized and undeputized men break into stores to steal guns and ammo.

Earlier, when he returned to the courthouse, light-skinned Walter White was inadvertently deputized. "Go shoot as many Niggers as you can," a particularly ruthless policeman told him. "You can shoot any Nigger you see, and the law will stand behind you."

Now Walter sidles away, then runs quickly to report this terrible news to folks in Greenwood. He stops first to warn Dick's aunt Damie, but she has already heard about Mr. Gurley's advice to leave town for the night. She tells Walter she's in a hurry to pack nightclothes and a change of day clothes for the trip to her aunt's house near Mingo.

"It's most near 8:00 p.m., and I wanna git out before it gits too dark," she tells Walter, shaking her head with worry. "I'm gonna ride the few miles to Mango Road in a mule wagon with some other families. But, I can't think now 'bout much other than what's gonna happen to my boy Dick."

*****

News of the Negro uprising spreads throughout white Tulsa as well as through Greenwood. By 9:00 p.m., events are moving faster than a runaway train. Many whites are coming downtown to watch the show. Many Blacks are making their getaway in total terror.

"Joleen, we've got to go. White folks are shooting Colored folks."

"Git your families out of here as fast as you can. They're killing Negroes uptown."

Black men load their families and a few belongings into cars and wagons, if they have them, and run for it as soon as they can. Some jump freight trains; others flee on foot. Many head north, some never to be heard from again. Young girls with frilly dresses laid out for their junior-senior prom now run for their lives. Wives beg their husbands not to fight. Some do run, but others stay to pepper the invaders of Greenwood with resistance as long as they can.

At 9:15 p.m., Harry Whiteside, a local white man who employs several Blacks at his foundry, runs into the Dreamland Theatre. "Turn these lights up," he yells. "The show's over." At that point, Blacks at the movie don't view white men as the enemy, so the lights go on, and everyone listens.

"A white mob is tryin' to lynch Dick Rowland at the courthouse," Whiteside tells the crowd. "The Black veterans have managed to stop them for now, but they've armed themselves and are shooting any Negroes they can find. Some of your people intend to fight, but I think that's a big mistake. If I was you, I'd run for cover, because hundreds of white men are comin' to get you." Terrified moviegoers push one another as they rush down the aisle to heed Whiteside's horrifying warning.

Not all whites are supportive. At almost the same time, a woman runs into the Rialto Theater on Main Street on the white side of the tracks and shrieks gleefully, "Nigger fight. Nigger fight." Another woman rushes into Getman's Drugstore across the street from the Majestic Theater where *Snowblind* has just finished playing. "There's a race riot goin' on," she yells to the white patrons. "Everyone, git out of here if you wanna join the fun."

Clarence Seward, father of three, is returning home from work in South Tulsa when a white gang starts chasing him. He runs for cover at the Royal Theater where *One Man in a Million* is playing. He is shot dead in the aisle by his pursuers, sending more frantic moviegoers screaming into the street.

By 9:30 p.m., Black riflemen set up a line of defense in a tall building at the southern edge of Greenwood Avenue. Other marksmen take up positions on North Elgin Street at Mt. Zion Church, the pride of the community completed just one month ago.

About half an hour later, white men light kerosene rags and throw them into the mostly wooden buildings of Greenwood. The winds carry the flames, and soon, almost all of Archer Street is on fire. The library is the first building of many to burst into flames.

Almost simultaneously, rumors spread that Mt. Zion is an arsenal for weapons and ammunition. Soon, the Tulsa unit of the National Guard riddles the church with bullets, torches the building, and shoots the Blacks pouring out through the sickening smoke.

By 10:00 p.m., it is impossible to tell the difference between police, vigilantes, and the local guard. The chaos creates a kind of cacophonous concert. Think Stravinsky's *The Rite of Spring*.

*****

Earlier that evening, Sheriff McCullough had gone home to rest for a while, leaving Police Chief John Gustafson in charge. Almost immediately, Gustafson directs his officers to round up all the Black men they can find, leaving Greenwood virtually defenseless.

Chief Gustafson is a square-jawed, potbellied man with a receding hairline. A former detective for the Tulsa Police Department, he had been fired because of collaboration with a Black drug dealer and sexual misconduct with another police officer's wife. McCullough was against hiring Gustafson when the job of police chief came open, but he was overruled by city fathers.

From the moment he is put in charge, Gustafson seems more concerned about what may happen to police headquarters than about what may happen to Dick Rowland. Located across the street from a gun store, the police headquarters is several blocks closer to Greenwood than to the courthouse where Dick is being held.

Gustafson orders police officers to mount two machine guns at Standpipe Hill, a knoll at the northernmost edge of Greenwood where the city's hundred-foot water tower was built fifteen years ago. Clearly, the police chief is planning for major trouble throughout the night and into the next day.

*****

Soon, it becomes obvious that the rampaging rioters have more in mind than lynching one Black teenager. Trucks and cars full of drunk, angry, armed white men blasting horns and shooting guns in all directions swarm over Greenwood. Many whites, including Harry Whiteside, try to get the marauders to stop but to no avail. The thugs systematically break into Black homes and businesses, drive the inhabitants out into the street, and go back inside to pillage and plunder.

A man carries out furniture and loads it into his truck, all the while complaining, "Damn Niggers got better stuff than most white people. Them animals don't deserve it." Some wives follow behind their husbands with pillowcases, sheets, shopping bags, and shipping crates. They steal furs, jewelry, silver, and china from the finer homes along the east side of Detroit, careful not to disrupt the white houses on the west side of the street. They break to pieces anything they don't want or can't carry, maliciously destroying cherished furnishings, keepsakes, and personal mementos.

"Lookie here, Wilma. These Niggers got a fox fur wrap. Don't I look good?"

"Oh, Betty Jean, I got me some diamonds—necklace, bracelet, and earrings—to match."

"Uppity Niggers. Where they git money for all this?"

"Ooh. I got me some fine china. I brought me a cardboard box so I could take some of this super fine crystal. I'm gonna wrap it in newspaper. Niggers ain't got no right to stuff this good."

"Wish I could carry off that chandelier."

"Here, break up that chandelier with this baseball bat and pull that phone outta the wall. They don't need it."

"Git them pitchers down off the wall and break 'em up. Burn that photo album and the Bible. Now let's set these rugs and furniture on fire before we move next door."

While the lead groups are looting and shooting, their comrades pile bedding, curtains, clothing, wooden furniture, papers, cooking oil, and other flammables inside or in front of homes and businesses. They douse the materials in kerosene before striking a match, then send up celebratory cheers as another home or business bursts into flames. Fire engines racing to the scene are turned back by the unruly mobs.

An elderly couple is shot in the back of their heads while saying their nightly prayers. One man is shot at the Harlan movie theater at the south end of Greenwood Avenue. Entire Black families are shot while running into their churches or, now ablaze, fleeing out of them.

Around 11:00 p.m., a group of police officers goes to the Stradford Hotel on North Greenwood. Proprietor J. B. Stradford, who returned to the hotel when the shooting started, is standing on his steps with a shotgun. "Good evening, Mr. Stradford," says the lead policeman.

"Not much good about it, Officer."

"You're right, JB. The violence is getting mighty close now, so you need to come with us for your own protection."

"I will under one condition," he responds. "Promise me you'll protect my hotel."

The officers make that promise, but as they drive Stradford away, others torch the hotel, just a small flash of the flames quickly engulfing Greenwood.

CHAPTER 7

And the Brutes Go On

June 1, 1921 (Early Morning to Dawn)

"My God, that sounds like a machine gun. What the..." Dick moans audibly.

"Shut your big black piehole, Nigger, or I'll shut it for you," a restless guard threatens as he bangs a tin cup on the cell bars just to rattle his terrified prisoner.

Dick is unable to sleep. The crowd around the courthouse has dwindled, but he can hear chaos in the distance. He can't stop thinking about his impending lynching, certain of the fate that awaits him. Still, he worries about what could be happening to his family and friends in Greenwood.

*****

The white rampage through Greenwood continues into the night. Well-intentioned whites, often at great personal peril, try to slow the destructive progression. Mostly, they are unable to do so. At times, Black defenders think they have stopped the onslaught, only to find new threats descending upon them. Violence erupts in nearly every quadrant, usually unbeknownst to those in other areas of Greenwood until it is too late.

Simon Scott, a Black lawyer, comes home to find his piano piled high in the street with his other furniture, but he cannot locate his wife and children. When he finds them days later, the family leaves Tulsa for good. John Williams rounds the corner of Greenwood and Archer in time to see his garage, with his family home above it, burst into flames. He leaves Tulsa that night after he learns from neighbors that his wife and children have escaped. He knows they will join him in Springfield, Illinois, where they have relatives. Williams is one of sixty-five Black men ultimately indicted for inciting the riot.

Clarence Brown hides in a crawl space at Dunbar Junior High School, but someone who sees him tips off the white rioters. They shoot into the crawl space, but they cannot tell if they have hit him or not, so they give up and torch the wooden school. Before his hiding place catches fire, Brown clambers out the back and starts running north. His wife never sees him again and believes he must have been killed. She wishes she could find out where he is buried—if he is buried.

Marauders besiege more and more Black homes. Flammable household belongings are torched. Sometimes, inhabitants flee before their houses are set ablaze. All too often, people are still inside and must somehow escape the suffocating smoke and crumbling structures or be burned alive. If they do get out, frenzied hoodlums either shoot to kill or force them to run for it, dodging gunfire as the thugs gleefully holler, "Dance little Nigger."

Roving gangs of whites with torches lighting their distorted, florid faces pour kerosene on Black men, women, and children they find on the street or hiding in alleys. Seemingly at random, they knock out teeth, poke out eyes, slap faces with their torches, or smash in heads before setting people on fire. They hang a crippled man with his crutches strapped to his arms. They find a Black veteran still in his uniform, set him on fire, and hoist him up a telephone pole with a rope wrapped around his body instead of his neck so he'll die more slowly.

Crowds of white people—men, women, and children—gather on a nearby hill overlooking the melee. It is just past midnight, but they still bring picnic baskets full of food to eat during the entertainment. Children run around screaming in glee while their parents snap souvenir photographs lit by the fiery night.

When the Tulsa unit of the National Guard arrives, the whites cheer, delighted at the spectacle. "City ought never to have sold damn Niggers property so close to the city," a critic of the Real Estate Exchange grumbles to his friends.

*****

Four white men in full cowboy regalia—hats, chaps, boots, vests, and string ties—ride down Greenwood Avenue on their giant bay horses. The horses weigh over a thousand pounds, and the black points on their manes, ears, tails, and lower legs make them look like avenging devils, the Four Horsemen of the Apocalypse. The cowboys charge the steeds through crowds of terrified Blacks and fire their guns at those running along the side, much like killing Indians in a Wild West movie or swatting flies.

One of the cowboys cracks a long whip, an evil-looking four-inch-wide piece of good leather some seven feet long with industrial tape around its wooden handle. The official whipping strap of the KKK, the last six inches are cut into ten slits, which makes the strap especially effective at slicing through skin and clothing. With the flick of a wrist, the cowboy draws blood, repeatedly ripping the flesh of fleeing Blacks or tripping them by tangling their ankles. As the horsemen wreak their havoc, small gangs of hoodlums break into businesses along Greenwood Avenue. They set fire to anything that will burn.

Two white men kick down the door at Alvin's Chili Parlor and storm in. They find four Black workers—one man and three women still in their aprons—crouched in the kitchen, afraid to go outside or run for their homes. The Blacks immediately throw their hands in the air, but the white men shoot them where they squat. The hoodlums pick up the cashbox before they pour kerosene over the bodies, stools, counters, booths, kitchen equipment, and floors. Then they set the once popular meeting place on fire.

A grocery owner pleads with a gang that has kicked in his door. "You can see I'm white. Why are you doing this to me?"

"Because you're a Jew and sell to Niggers," replies one of the men as he torches the grocery.

All four of the topless Ford Model Ts in Simon Berry's Taxi Service are destroyed. Blacks seek sanctuary in their churches, but white ruffians torch and burn every one of them nearly to the ground. Terrified, people are shot as they run out of the blazing churches, usually with their hands in the air. One Black church is spared because the mob mistakenly believes it is a white church on the edge of Greenwood.

A group of eight Black women are gathered in the basement of the Second Baptist Church to pray. A white vigilante named Leroy Butler calmly walks in and shoots the women, then signals his comrades to set fire to the building. Gary Smith, a reluctant member of the gang, hangs back. He had tried but failed to dissuade Leroy from going into the church. Now the deed is done, and his companions rush in to finish the job.

Around 1:00 a.m., Dr. A. C. Jackson goes across the street on a house call to check on the wife of his neighbor, retired judge John Oliphant. Dr. J. assures his own wife he won't be gone long, brushing her cheek with a quick kiss. As he leaves his patient's home thirty minutes later, a gang of white men approach. Dr. J. has a police escort, his hands in the air, and a white handkerchief is tied around one arm, signifying neutrality.

"Don't hurt him," Judge Oliphant yells. "This is Doctor Jackson."

But a white trash teenager shoots anyway. The gentle Dr. J. is shot and killed. The last thing he sees is his house on fire. He doesn't know his wife and children have escaped.

*****

The harrying hordes grow in number, arms, and drunkenness throughout the night. Some police officers and special deputies are not merely complicit in the multiple heinous crimes throughout Greenwood. They are frequently the perpetrators who actually commit the torture, murder, and looting.

Police are scattered across Tulsa, including in white neighborhoods where poor whites break into the homes of rich whites who have Blacks working and living there. Thugs pull the servants out in their nightclothes, load them onto trucks, and signal the police to haul them to one of the makeshift internment camps quickly set up just hours ago. No effort is made by the police to stop any of these activities. They are there only to protect white property and round up Blacks.

Loud gunshots erupt from two machine guns installed earlier by police chief John Gustafson on Standpipe Hill, a knoll at the northernmost edge of Greenwood. Dozens of Black bodies lie silenced at the bottom of the hill. Nearby residents later report seeing bodies loaded like cordwood on trucks and wagons and then hauled away.

The staccato machine-gun fire pierces the night as police mow down Black men hiding behind nearby trees until they raise a white flag in surrender. The terrified captives are paraded hands up to one of the newly minted camps—perhaps Convention Hall at 105 West Brady Street or McNulty Baseball Park at Tenth and Elgin or the fairgrounds at Twenty-First and Yale or some other South Tulsa venue paid for by taxpayer dollars.

The eruptions of gunfire, kitchens exploding, blasting horns, shrieks, cries, moans, and a hurricane of hellfire create a sorrowful crescendo of chaos and calamity. Conspicuously absent are sounds from the sirens of rescue vehicles. Throngs of whites prevent ambulances from assisting wounded Blacks and firefighters from dousing flames. Rescue is not on the way.

Unfounded rumors spread through South Tulsa that truckloads of Blacks are arriving from other places. "Niggers are trying to take over the city," a breathless white man tells police. Officers rush out to block the roads.

*****

By 2:00 a.m., the four-story Middle States Milling Company, located just south of the Frisco tracks across from Greenwood Avenue, has been taken over by vigilantes. From this vantage point, whites fire indiscriminately through shattered windows into the very heart of North Tulsa. They take incoming fire from Black defenders, but not enough to stop the carnage. Around 3:00 a.m., after frantic pleas from Tulsa officials, the governor finally calls out the National Guard. About a hundred special troops board the train in Oklahoma City at 5:00 a.m., headed for Tulsa.

As fatigue sets in on both sides, quiet seems to return to Greenwood. Those who have not fled fall into an exhausted, uneasy sleep. Greenwood seems at peace. The white invasion has been halted, and the Negro uprising averted. Or so it seems.

CHAPTER 8

It Ain't Over Yet

June 1, 1921 (Dawn to Midafternoon)

Many Blacks hope dawn will bring a lasting peace and an opportunity to clean up whatever mess there is. Most have no idea of the extent of damage and death that has already transpired in parts of Greenwood. They are just glad for what seems like peace and quiet.

As dawn breaks, white gangs gather in their denim shirts and overalls, armed to the teeth with pistols and shotguns. They have been planning and drinking all night, passing around bottles of whiskey and choc beer, a milky, highly intoxicating home brew. They have also been trading guns and ammo to secure the proper-gauged ammo needed for their stolen guns. Now they are solidifying plans to invade Greenwood.

There are basically three main vigilante groups, now collectively more than ten thousand strong. One group is hiding behind the Frisco freight depot south of Greenwood Avenue. Another is waiting by the Frisco and Santa Fe passenger station near First and Cincinnati. The third group is at the Katy passenger depot just west of the western edge of Greenwood. Meanwhile, smaller bands of armed whites rove the streets, causing as much trouble as they can. Sometimes, they meet resistance from Blacks and, occasionally, from a few helpful whites.

It is still dark at around 5:00 a.m. when a small group of white men in a Franklin Automobile drive up to the rabble at the Frisco freight depot and holler, "What the hell are you waiting for? Let's go get 'em." No one joins, but they drive straight toward the heart of Greenwood anyway. Later that morning, their bullet-riddled vehicle and dead bodies are found at the intersection of Archer and Frankfort.

At approximately 6:00 a.m., a strange whistle sounds, and thousands of armed white men suddenly overrun Greenwood from several directions, robbing and beating any Black man, woman, or child they find. At the Katy depot, dozens of cars join the mobs heading east on Brady and Cameron Streets. Firing their guns and blasting their horns, the invaders form a steel circle of automobiles and guns surrounding Greenwood.

*****

Virginia Small asks her brother Bobby Jr. why in the hell he wants to go down to Niggertown so early in the morning with all the chaos going on. Without answering, he leaves in his father's new Chrysler convertible to pick up Jasper Hicks and a couple of other buddies to go joyriding toward Greenwood.

Hiram Porter, the blind, legless Black veteran, is sitting on his wagon on the boardwalk on Main Street, just the other side of the tracks from Greenwood Avenue. He's whistling like he always does—"I ain't got nobody..."—mostly oblivious to the early morning mayhem. Beside him sit his pencil box and money cup.

The car slowly pulls up beside him. His whistle gets softer on the final line—"And nobody cares for me." One of Bobby Jr.'s nasty, loud, and laughing friends throws a choc bottle near Hiram. It is a heavy bottle. It rolls along the sidewalk, echoing in the silence. The whistling stops; the bottle rolls. The bottle thrower and his back seat drinking partner leave the vehicle and stumble up the steps to threaten the defenseless veteran.

"Aw, boys, y'all don't need to hurt me," he pleads, now fully aware that there are gunshots, screams, and even machine gun fire just a few blocks away. Jasper jumps out of the front seat and heads straight for Hiram. After rushing to Sarah's side during the incident at the Drexel Building and being rebuffed as usual, he feels especially angry and aims to get revenge wherever he can find it. Coldly, he caresses the roll of rope in his hands, perhaps as he had hoped to do with the strawberry-blond beauty he will never have.

"What goin' on, boss?" Hiram asks. Wordlessly, Jasper ties the rope tightly to the fender of Mr. Small's convertible. Then he methodically and tightly ties the rope around the crippled vet's longer stump. He tries to resist, but Jasper backhands him hard across the face, and Hiram topples off his wagon and hits the ground. Jasper finishes his unholy knot with a foot on his victim's chest.

"Har, har, har. Look at him, shaking like a bitch shittin' peach pits," Jasper squeals. The three bullies jump back into the convertible, still laughing as Bobby Jr. revs the engine and yanks Hiram down the steps and into the street. They drag him up Main Street where he screams, choking on the blood in his throat as his head bashes against bricks and steel streetcar rails. The drunk punks shriek convulsively when he soils himself and bark out hard laughter as they gleefully execute their murderous torture.

Hiram's agonized screams can be heard for the several hours it takes until he goes limp. The four buddies continue dragging his corpse across the tracks and onto Greenwood Avenue to the sounds of shooting, looting, and whooping white louts.

*****

While hoodlums continue to besiege Greenwood from the south and west, bullets start falling from the sky, looking to some like little black birds. Six civilian aircraft swoop down over Greenwood, firing on every Black person they can target and dropping some type of incendiary device, perhaps nitroglycerine, turpentine balls, or coal oil. The white pilots, several of them oil barons or employees rich from the black gold of nearby gushers, drop their bombs onto the tops of buildings, including churches and private homes still left standing despite the assault from the ground.

Circling Greenwood like vultures, the double-winged flying machines frighten people in the streets below. They are like devilish dragonflies diving down, delivering death and destruction. Three are newer metal planes; three are older models covered in canvas. Some are commercial barnstorming planes, ones that earn their owners a living by charging for rides at county fairs. Some were bought in Kansas, which had recently become a hub for flight. A couple of planes had come from an auction in England of World War I surplus.

Incindiary devices falling from the sky catch men, women, and children and set them ablaze. People run while burning alive. The streets are filled with smoke, fire, and frightened Black folks fleeing their homes in tumultuous terror. The bombing makes Tulsa the first American city to be attacked from the air.

*****

After firing all night, Otis Gibbs has taken advantage of the brief silence to grab a short nap. Now he reloads his shotgun and again fires south at the vigilantes who have overtaken the Middle States Milling building. He can see white men in the broken windows shooting Black men, women, and children in the street. He reloads and reloads, shooting as quickly as possible at the gangsters in front of his Red Wing Hotel.

Otis sees a white man walk out of the hotel in a full-length leopard skin coat he recognizes as belonging to Ernestine Burns. Another man has a Victrola in his hands. Still, others carry plush chairs from the lobby. Once the hotel is plundered, the mob starts throwing fiery rags into the building, and Otis runs for it. Unfortunately, he runs directly into the hands of a white gang, who beat him and then force him into a line of beleaguered Blacks being marched toward the detention center.

Stumbling up Greenwood, Otis is shattered by what he sees: whites looting and burning Black businesses with impunity—Mr. Ferguson's drugstore, Mrs. Walker's beauty parlor, J. T. Presley's restaurant, Alvin's Chili Parlor where he used to meet his wife before they married, Williams Garage, and the confectionary next door—while police officers look on and do nothing or, worse, assist in the destruction.

As Otis is marched up the street in a long line of prisoners, hands in the air, he thinks about the crowded Thursday nights on this very street—Greenwood Avenue, the heart and soul of the Black community, now in chaos and flames.

On maids' day off, girls who worked as domestics for wealthy whites in South Tulsa would come home to show off their most fashionable attire. Some of the more daring sported sleeveless dresses, but most wore V-necks or boatnecks with long or elbow-length sleeves in pastel or soft lavenders and pink floral prints. Pleated skirts at ankle length or just below the knee were the order of the day. He loved how the girls would promenade down Greenwood Avenue from Archer to Pine and back again. They would sashay in a stylish display of their good fortune: fabulous nails, perfectly matched jewelry, and hair done up neatly with a little fluff they could tamp down for work the next day.

A smile almost crosses his lips as he imagines the young girls gathering with friends to giggle and flirt with young men also dressed to the nines. The fellows are like peacocks preening, prancing, and almost dancing with the nice girls they'll never meet at the County Line. Up and down Greenwood Avenue, the young people circle one another in a spirited stroll, stopping to chat, stopping for an ice cream, happy to be alive, employed, and free for one day. Even the caddies, greenkeepers, and yardmen who don't get days off dress up as best they can and join in the festivities. But Otis knows those days have literally gone up in flames. Today, fear and chaos reign where joy and pride ruled just days before.

*****

Emboldened by their successes, the hooligans continue throughout the morning to brutalize Blacks and march them, many still in nightclothes, into makeshift internment camps. Or if patience wears thin, they just shoot them dead as they march with hands in the air. A white woman later reports she saw wagons full of dead Black bodies dumped into mass graves. Others report seeing bodies thrown into the river. Some of the dead are Black men of means with friends in white Tulsa, but the rowdy rabble, blind with rage and choc, is either incapable of making the distinction or wholeheartedly disinclined to do so.

A group of trembling Blacks hides in a wooden water tank in the alley behind Vadan's Pool Hall despite their fear it may burn up in the holocaust that is now Greenwood. About half an hour later, a small band of brutes opens the lid; and upon seeing what's inside, they keep shooting until not a body is moving.

Hiding in the relative safety of the luxurious Dreamland Theatre, Harry Smithson, a Black carpenter from Muskogee, shelters from the clamor and chaos outside. As horns blare, he mutters to himself, "These honkies are sure living up to their name this morning." But by 9:00 a.m., the seats, curtains, and carpets of his hiding place are ablaze. The smoke is stifling, and he flees, hoping to find safe transportation back home. It takes him three days of hiding and running and walking, mostly at night, to cover the fifty-two miles back to Muskogee.

Newly deputized degenerates are especially cruel as they capture and torture unarmed Blacks. They drag one man behind a truck with a noose around his neck. They burn others alive. They strip and violently rape women and young girls, leaving some of them naked, bleeding, and mortified in the streets. They throw Blacks out of upper-floor windows of boarding houses, often to be trampled by the wheels of oncoming cars and wagons.

A police officer on a motorcycle has tied a rope through the belt loops of several Black men and is pulling them behind his bike toward the new fairgrounds incarceration center more than six miles into South Tulsa. A black Buick filled with white ruffians ploughs into the line of Blacks, leaving dead and wounded of all ages in their wake. The murderous delinquents laugh hysterically as they speed away.

John Little, a Black entrepreneur, tries to protect his family business, the popular Ross and Little Café, until it is overtaken by the sheer number of rapacious whites. He runs north along the Midland Valley tracks with other desperate refugees. Their exodus looks like lines of ants trudging north in hopes of finding a safe haven. In their panicked flight, some of the refugees mumble the words Uncle Hiram used to say: "At some point, you decide you're either gonna live or you're gonna die." They hope to live.

*****

For the most part, police officers continue to assist the white hoodlums, often joining in the burning and looting and rarely protecting Black people or their property. Despite the negligence of police and other local officials, there are efforts by whites to provide Black refugees safe havens in their homes in South Tulsa. Some had even set up cots in small spare rooms the day before, expecting trouble from what happened at the courthouse.

Mr. Oberholtzer, city superintendent of public schools, arrives at the convention center to vouch for the Black teachers held there. White teachers at Central High take the Black female teachers from Washington High School into their homes. The Black male teachers are housed and fed at Washington High.

Two white churches, First Presbyterian Church and the Catholic Holy Family Cathedral, feed and shelter victims of the massacre. After hearing about what is going on in Greenwood, Virginia Small, in an uncharacteristic act of kindness, defies her callous father and brother by rushing down to First Presbyterian to help. But the brutish actions of the mob overrule the kindnesses.

By the time the National Guard arrives from Oklahoma City around noon—after they stop to have their lunch—most of Greenwood is burning. The guardsmen help put out fires. They systematically round up Blacks who have survived and march them off to the detention camps "for their protection." By the end of the day, more than six thousand Blacks (from a population of approximately ten thousand) are interned at the ballpark, Convention Hall, and fairgrounds. For at least two months, Blacks cannot be on the streets without a large card that says POLICE PROTECTION.

POLICE PROTECTION

NAME ....

ADDRESS ....

Approved ....

AMERICAN RED CROSS
CLARK FIELD, Chairman

AMERICAN
RED CROSS

Refugee Card

R. R. TRANSPORTATION

To ....

CITY TRANSPORTATION

To ....

EMPLOYED

At ....

SHELTERED

At ....

BED AND BEDDING

....

MEDICAL AID

At ....

By ....

PROVISIONS ISSUED

June

CLOTHING FURNISHED

Police Protection Card (front)
and Refugee Card (back) required for Greenwood citizens
to wear on streets for months after Massacre
courtesy of the Tulsa Historical Society

What was one of the most affluent African American communities in the United States on May 31 literally lies in ashes by the end of the day, June 1, 1921.

CHAPTER 9

So Damn Lucky

Spring 1997

Grandchildren bless the lives of Hattie and Lucy today. Hattie had a happy marriage to Andrew Rogers for nearly forty years. He was a kind, responsible man, not wild about church but a good father to the two boys, Ernest and Harvey. Andrew almost never drank and came home and washed up for supper every night. He treated Hattie like a queen and always took good care of the boys, going to all their games and making sure they dressed well and spoke respectfully to their elders.

Lucy met Harold Wilson at Howard law school, at a café where they both worked weekends. Soon after graduation, she convinced him to start a law practice with her in Tulsa, where they raised their two children. Nola, the older one, was an RN who became a missionary and decided not to have children. Elroy made up for that by giving them two wonderful grandchildren.

Harold was a churchgoing man, a fine lawyer, and an attentive father. He passed away just over five years ago, right after his second grandchild, little Julius, was born. Shortly thereafter, Lucy moved in with Hattie, whose husband, Andrew, had died a few years prior. These days, the two old ladies thank their lucky stars that those three boys blessed their mommas with the boisterous little grandchildren they love like crazy.

Almost all members of the two families stayed in or near the Greenwood area and strongly supported their community. Sunday suppers were family dinners, at first always at either Hattie's or Lucy's but in later years rotating between the four remaining households. Tables were set with care, and grace was always said by the head of whichever household was hosting supper. Even Andrew, when it had been his turn, would recite a brief blessing, but only because he thought it set a good example, not because he believed any of that superstition, he would remind Hattie after supper.

Usually, fried chicken and mashed potatoes and gravy were on the table, along with biscuits and more gravy, greens or okra or corn in season, and tomatoes all summer. For dessert, there was fruit pie or cobbler with fresh fruit when available, sometimes with homemade ice cream, but always dessert. The new electric ice cream maker was a welcome addition, but Hattie often said it wasn't as much fun as the old crank style.

Hattie and granddaughter Tuletta baked chocolate chip cookies, in the winter, especially. Occasionally, Lucy's granddaughter Pearl would pitch in, but she never really seemed to like cooking so much. This always brought back happy memories to Hattie from when she and her aunt Damie would bake cookies in the Adams kitchen before the Depression forced them to leave Kansas City.

For both Hattie and Lucy, their greatest pleasure had been watching their grandchildren grow up and learn to be kind and generous as well as smart. All five fathers—Andrew, Harold, Ernest, Harvey, and Elroy—had been strict disciplinarians, not cruel or unkind, and fortunately, none of them was a big drinker. Both women had loved their own children growing up, but even mommas had to be a bit strict and often didn't have enough time to play with them. Now the antics of their grands are a complete joy, and they have more time to play with the little dickens. Full of life, the children bedevil and delight the old ladies, who met at Booker T. Washington High School so many years ago.

*****

The lifelong friends have achieved so much more than most in their community could dare to dream. Sometimes, the guilt weighs heavily upon them. Occasionally, they talk about it. Mostly, they focus on the positive or the humorous, especially while watching their grandchildren play. "Remember when we thought artichokes were weeds growing in the yard? Now we're eating them like delicacies," Hattie says, laughing.

Growing up during the Depression had not been a picnic for anyone. It hit the Black population especially hard, even in Greenwood. A lot had been rebuilt since 1921, but most of the houses were without running water or indoor facilities in the 1930s. Electricity was hit or miss, almost no one had telephones or automobiles, and even doctors and lawyers walked most places to save gas.

Neither family had money for cheer squad uniforms or band instruments, but both girls showed up for every game and supported their teams—those Hornets. Hattie knew her daddy had played football for the Hornets, albeit briefly, and it made her feel closer to him somehow to cheer for the team, his team. She once saw a photo of him in his football uniform in a Washington High yearbook, but she could never find the original photo. That yearbook was deep in the bowels of the school library, and she rarely saw it. To this day, she thinks he was the handsomest man she ever saw, next to Andrew, of course.

"We had to work after school, but at least we could go to school. So many couldn't," Hattie continues reminiscing with Lucy as they watch the children play. "They had to work as much as they could to help feed the family, and the family was usually too large to support. I think that's when I first realized that large families were part of what was holding Blacks back."

"Same for poor whites. Daddies out of work took to drinking and roughing up their kids and wives. We were probably better off with no daddies around," Lucy says, causing Hattie to wince. "I know we love our babies, but it's hard to share that love with so many when you have to work all the time just to put food on the table, clothes on their backs."

"I remember when times started to get a little better, most Blacks still couldn't get decent jobs and got no help with schooling. Parents, if there were two, worked multiple jobs, and the kids worked too just to keep body and soul together."

"I remember when we couldn't go into white Tulsa or at least couldn't go into any of the nice shops without being followed. We were rudely, if barely, served. Now we can shop at Miss Jackson's and have lunch at the Wild Fork."

"If you don't mind the occasional stares of superiority," Hattie retorts. "When I walk through the greater Greenwood district today—what there is left of it—it makes me sad that there are still so many children in raggedy clothes, dirty, uneducated. Many houses are little more than shacks. Of course, most of the district has been ripped apart by that interstate highway, and most Blacks with any means have moved out."

"I still feel loyal to Greenwood, although I know we probably should have moved out years ago, financially speaking," Lucy admits. "The schools are much worse than when our children were in school and when you were teaching. If we hadn't helped send these grandkids to private school before they reached high school, I guess our sons and their families would have had to move to better districts because busing was not always the best solution in Tulsa, in my opinion."

*****

School is out for Easter, and the kids are feeling euphoric to be free and to be with their beloved grandmothers, who will dutifully spoil them rotten. The two women often complain about the weather, but not today when the warm spring morning sun is shining and the grandchildren are full of piss and vinegar.

Hide-and-seek is always a favorite game in the large front yard filled with shrubs and trees and other excellent nooks and crannies. The older children, Pearl and Tuletta, order younger Melvin and Julius to follow the rules as they make them up. The act of hiding—deciding where to hide, discarding that decision, and staking claim to another—all the while the child called IT is counting is hilarity itself but does not compare to the shrieks of pure joy when someone is found.

After hours of play, the children are thrilled when the pizza and sodas arrive, goodies their parents almost never let them have. But then they must nap, resisting until sleep overcomes them and a much-needed rest is had by all.

Rocking on the front porch, the old ladies continue to reminisce. "We've been so damn lucky, Hattie," Lucy tells her dear friend. "We had parents who were able to ensure we had a chance and good husbands who believed in education. Education is the key, and most of our people have not had that chance."

"Your rich white daddy and my dear aunt Damie and Momma made sure there was money enough for us to break free. We've done everything we can for our children and these grandchildren, but I sure wish we could do something for the rest."

Both women are grateful that they had uncharacteristically small families and that their children did the same. They loved their babies, but they made a pact in high school not to have too many when they saw how large families struggled. Plus, they decided children could be better cared for in smaller families. Out of respect, they have always been careful not to proselytize on this point.

"You did a great deal for those kids at Washington High, Hattie. Don't sell yourself short. You know you went way above and beyond normal teachers' duties, and every one of them and their parents knew and appreciated that and you."

"You know I loved those kids and wanted the world for them. I've been so proud to see many of them go on to college, but I do wish more could go. And the whole community is grateful to you and Harold for so much pro bono work and for mentoring and sponsoring so many of our young people."

"I just wish we could do more."

The black Pontiac gleams in the driveway, testament to the good luck Lucy claims and so appreciates. So does the neatly manicured lawn and well-kept bungalow, often called a Prairie Schooner, that Hattie and Andrew retired to and that she now shares with her dearest friend.

*****

Hattie and Andrew retired to Reservoir Hill when urban renewal started destroying what they loved the most about Greenwood. Across the front of the house is a small porch with a nice brick railing and concrete steps leading up to it. When the boys aren't around, granddaughters Tuletta and Pearl like to play pirates on the porch swing using yardsticks for swords, just like Hattie used to do so many years ago in Kansas City.

Like most homes in the neighborhood, the bungalow she shares with Lucy has two bedrooms and two baths—good for the old ladies and especially useful when the grandchildren come over. The one-car garage is used for storage along with a full basement for additional storage, the laundry, and indoor hide-and-seek. There is a separate dining room and a kitchen nook for breakfast, which the grandkids especially love because "it feels like a booth at the café."

Education, temperance, frugality, faith, and family are the five points on these ladies' North Star, and they have followed them religiously. These virtues—plus regulating the size of their families, hard work, and a little bit of luck—have led them to a Promised Land they want to make possible for all Greenwood children. But how?

CHAPTER 10

Making the Case

Fall 1997

After weeks of phone calls, coffees, teas, breakfasts, and lunches, Hattie and Lucy are in Rep. Don Ross's Tulsa office to meet with Wilbur McNeely and report their progress on arranging dozens of depositions with survivors. "Many have photographs to back up their stories," Lucy proclaims proudly as she lays several documents on the legislative aide's conference table.

"That's just great, ladies. The interviews and depositions are starting right away. Senator Maxine Horner and Representative Ross have a bill ready to go before the state legislature to commission this report." Wilbur goes on to recount for Hattie and Lucy what he and his staff have learned after examining the minutes from Tulsa City Commission meetings between 1920 and 1932, newspaper articles, court records, insurance records, and multiple other documents.

"We discovered what we already knew—many claims for property damage during the riots were paid to whites, but every claim by a Black home or business owner was denied. Claims were promptly and meticulously filed but unceremoniously and routinely denied if the claimant was Black. White gun store owners got compensated for the guns stolen to murder our people but nothing for Blacks whose businesses and homes were looted and incinerated."

Though hardly surprised, Lucy can barely hide her disgust. "That's reprehensible," she says through clenched teeth.

"And although we don't have all the minutes from their meetings," Wilbur continues, "we know from stories in the newspapers at the time that business interests wanted the land immediately around the Frisco depot for a passenger and full railhead facility, and they wanted all of Greenwood for a white commercial district. The articles are shamelessly right there in both the *World* and the *Tribune*." Wilbur points to a folder on the conference table labeled Chamber of Commerce, July 1, 1921.

"We have minutes from this meeting which state that immediate steps should be taken to build a union station and terminal because the fire made a site available for this purpose. We also know that immediately after the Riot, the Real Estate Exchange reevaluated the land and offered Negroes pennies on the dollar for what their property was worth.

"From other sources, we know that police officers deputized only white men and arrested only Black men, putting them in camps as fast as they could. And we can document that six airplanes piloted by whites flew over the area, making Tulsa the first city in America to be bombed from the air."

After pausing to let that sink in, Lucy adds findings from her and Hattie's own research and conversations with survivors: "Wilbur, we also know that the city immediately passed a fire ordinance, which made it mandatory to build only with stone and concrete in Greenwood. These materials were prohibitively expensive. Other laws were designed to force our people to move. There were no insurance payments, and no bank would lend us money to rebuild, but we rebuilt anyway."

"Well, a lot of thanks goes to B. C. Franklin, working out of a tent for months to get that fire ordinance ruled unconstitutional," Hattie chimes in.

Bringing the focus back to why they are there, Wilbur tells them, "The goal of the Commission and Report is to hold public hearings and invite the media so everyone will know what went on all those years ago. Our report and the hearings must clearly lay out what happened. Just be aware, ladies, some folks will not believe the truth."

"Wilbur, people's livelihoods were stolen from them," Lucy responds solemnly. "These were human beings, real people, our people. Businesses, robbed and ruined. Life savings and life works, incinerated. As you know, more than fifteen hundred houses and businesses were destroyed—the Black hospital, library, hotels, and nearly every one of our twenty-four churches. Hopes and dreams, not just deferred or denied but decimated. Families, destroyed or nearly so. Businesses people had worked and saved to build, all up in smoke.

"Let me tell you about some of our people who lost everything," Lucy continues. "Take the Williams, for example. Their garage, theater, soda shop, and four rooming houses all paid for, all reduced to ashes. Or the Johnsons—their café, home, and boarding house. Or the Richardsons' seventeen rooming houses or the Harlans' theater or the Jones' grocery store, which, by the way, was owned by Representative Ross's maternal grandfather. The stately brick homes of the doctors and other professionals along Detroit were largely still standing but looted and irreparably damaged in most cases, I could go on and on."

Hattie, always the former teacher, pleads with Wilbur. "Young people lost their childhoods, their innocence. They had not thought of white people as the enemy before then. They missed defining moments in their high school careers, and one of the most serious problems then, as now, was the state of Negro education. How can our children prosper if they can't get a decent education? We need more teachers, better books, and scholarships, especially college scholarships. Can you get that into the recommendations?"

The two ladies are almost always upbeat and optimistic, but when the destruction of Greenwood is the subject, a bitter fog of grief, shame, anger, and uncharacteristic helplessness nearly suffocates them. They cannot uncry the years of tears. That well has run dry, leaving an aching hunger—not only for revenge but ultimately for justice.

After a somber pause, Wilbur resumes. "I think we have a good case, and we have the votes to get the Commission and Report funded. We haven't started writing the report yet, but we certainly believe, as you do, that education is key. I'm not sure what, if anything, will happen after the Oklahoma Commission and Report. I believe this will have to be resolved at the federal level. I don't believe Tulsa or Oklahoma officials will ever agree to pay reparations. I'm surprised Florida did. The state is full of crackers, just like Oklahoma."

"At a minimum," Lucy sums up, "compensation should be paid for actual damages, literally millions in today's dollars—the schools, the churches, homes, and businesses. Nearly three million dollars in insurance claims by Blacks were denied while claims by whites were honored. I guess pain and suffering are not likely to play into the equation because white people don't think Black people feel pain."

The report, commissioned in 1997, was finally presented to the governor of Oklahoma in 2001.

CHAPTER 11

Rendezvous with Destiny

June 1, 1921 (Late Afternoon)

Within a day, Dick is released. Sarah did not come to file charges. His right eye is badly swollen where one of the police guards had hit him. His yellow silk shirt is peppered with bloodstains. His once shiny boots are encrusted with red mud from the sodden earth around the courthouse.

Cautiously, Dick turns east and walks the seven blocks of white businesses along Sixth Street. Then he zigzags north toward home. In the white district, he notices that gun and hardware stores have been looted, and there's rubble in the streets, but most buildings are relatively untouched. "Maybe it wasn't as bad as it sounded," he hopes.

When he crosses the tracks into Greenwood, he cannot believe his eyes. He is shocked at what he sees or, rather, doesn't see as he looks up and down Greenwood Avenue and at all the cross streets. The Gurley Hotel; Netherland barbershop; Welcome grocery; Liberty Café; Elliot Hooker's clothing store; Bryant's drugstore; the Double D Lounge; the El Dorado, where the greats used to jam after their gigs in the white hotels; the pool halls, including Spann's, his favorite; and Williams Garage, confectionary, and rooming house—all gone, nowhere to be seen, just ashes, embers, and debris.

Dick heard from the guards that a white employee of the Black-owned *Tulsa Star* had died while setting fire to the paper that had employed him for years. "Serves him right," he thinks. What he does see makes him want to vomit. Greenwood has crumbled into a sea of dying embers. Valuables, heirlooms, pictures, and other family stories litter the streets. Burnt bodies are strewn across streets and alleys. What once was a lively community, his community, his home, has been reduced to ashes.

Dick is overcome with a greater sense of grief and shame than he has ever known. He cannot fathom what could have gone on here. A heavy depression nearly knocks him to the street. "What have I done? What did I start? How did this happen here in Tulsa?" he sobs.

In jail, when he learned about what had happened to Uncle Hiram, he nearly got sick and had to swallow hard to fight the bile rising up his throat. Now he is broken and ashamed. Pangs of guilt rack his body as he almost breaks down, knowing that he was the spark that ignited the inferno. He is certain that several of his friends and cousins have perished in the fires or have been shot or ended up in detention camps or worse.

He heard that his aunt Damie has survived and that her house is still standing, the house where he spent most of his life. Figuring he must leave Tulsa, Dick knew he will miss it all but felt sure none of the living or the dead would miss him. Now he truly understands what Uncle Hiram used to say: "Ain't no greater burden than knowin' you done wrong to folks you love."

"Hey. You're Dick Rowland, ain't you?" An elderly woman rouses him from his pity party, yelling and hitting him with her purse. "Are you proud of yourself? You donkey. You single-handedly destroyed Greenwood, you dumb Nigger." A gathering crowd hurls insults left and right.

> We'd a been better off if that mob hadda lynched ya.
>
> What were you doin' messin' 'round with a white gal anyway? Ain't you got a lick a sense? You know what always come of that. Now we all gotta pay the price for your foolishness.
>
> We got nuthin' now thanks to you, Dick Rowland. Cain't you see what you done? Barely

one brick standing on another. Churches, houses of worship, burned in a living hell that you caused. You proud of yourself, Nigger?

What you doin' showin' yer face 'round here, boy?

You git outta here afore we do to you what dem white boys shoulda done.

We had a life before you ruined it, ruined Greenwood, our homes, our families, you selfish pig.

Why in the world would you come back here? You ain't welcome here. Never.

Damn fool.

Complete idiot.

The crowd is growing larger and angrier by the minute. People are ominously circling and crowding closer to Dick. "Who do you think you are? Your aunt Damie raised you better 'n that."

"And so I did," Dicks hears Aunt Damie yell from the edge of the crowd—a sound so sweet that he wants to weep like a little boy. "Now all y'all git and leave this boy alone. He didn't burn down our town. Dem white thugs did with help from the police, the sheriff, the National Guard, and some airplanes. So you go on, git. Leave my boy alone."

She roughly grabs Dick by the arm and pulls him home, to the battered house filled with shattered glass and debris she must have been trying to clean up since late morning. "Now you tell me the truth, boy, and you tell me right now. Why were you runnin' outta that elevator, and why was Sarah Page faintin'? I know you been messin' 'round with her out at the County Line. I told you she was trouble."

"Cain't talk now, Aunt Damie. We gotta git outta this place afore someone—Colored or white—kills us. Pack up and meet me at the corner of Greenwood and Archer in forty-five minutes, where the Webb hotel is…or was." He gives her a quick hug and darts out of the house.

Sneaking down the back alleys and staying out of sight the best he can, Dick circles back to white Tulsa's northern edge, just across the tracks from Greenwood. He finally reaches the back of the dingy small boarding house on Third and Elgin, four blocks from the Drexel Building and two blocks from a prostitutes' promenade. He raps quietly on the window. Sarah looks out and quickly pulls him inside.

"Oh, my sweet Dick, I never meant for any of this to happen. Can you ever forgive me? I was just scared and afraid you were runnin' off from me because you didn't want this baby."

"We'll talk 'bout that later," he says as they embrace. "Right now, you gotta pack up your things 'cause we gotta git outta here before someone kills us, and it may be a Nigger mob this time. And yes, I want the baby, our baby. You started faintin', and I started runnin' to get some smelling salts. Then I seen dat bunch of white boys waitin' at the elevator and just took off."

Dick looks around the tiny apartment, Mrs. B's Boarding House, their love nest—the small bed where his feet always hung off, a hot plate by the filthy sink, chipped white paint on a small plywood chest with two short drawers, a broken mirror lying on top of a stained paper doily, no closet, two blouses hanging on the door threshold, and a bathroom down the hall. He remembers the great times he and Sarah had dazzling everyone with their moves on the dance floor out at the County Line, then coming back here to love all night until time to go to work. But his wistful ruminations are cut short by the urgency of the moment.

*****

Sarah hurriedly stuffs a few things into a pillowcase, the only suitcase she has. She casts a long, last look around, remembering the sweetness of their time together in this room—the soft murmurs of love, dreams shared, hushed laughter. He is the most thoughtful man she has ever met, she would often tell him, generous and chivalrous, sometimes to a fault. She smiles but knows she must stop her reminiscing.

"It ain't much," Sarah tells Dick, pointing to her barely bulging pillowcase.

"Don't matter, honey baby. We gotta git. I got us a ride and three jobs workin' for nice white folks in Kansas City. It ain't perfect, but right now, it a lot safer for us than Tulsey." Cautiously, they climb out of the back window they had crawled into on so many happy nights.

"Three jobs, sweet D?" Sarah asks as they run.

"Yeah. Aunt Damie's comin' with us. Don't want her gittin' hurt by anyone mad at me. And she can help with the baby. She's meetin' us at Greenwood and Archer in fifteen minutes. If anythin' slows me down, you run on with Aunt Damie. Jimmy borrowed his boss's car, a green Model T, and he'll be there 'bout the same time. I plan on bein' with you, but if somethin' do happen to slow me down, you go on. I'll meet you in Kansas City, where we'll give our baby a better life."

"Dick, what's goin' to happen to slow..." Sarah stops midsentence as a gang of trashy white toughs descends upon them. They don't recognize Sarah, who slips away while they harass Dick.

"Looks like we got ourselves some unfinished business here, boys," snarls one of the thugs. Sarah hears a scuffle. She is panicked and torn between wanting to help Dick and following his orders to meet him in Kansas City—for their baby. She doesn't dare turn around, and she rushes to meet Jimmy and Aunt Damie.

*****

Dick tries to run, but one of the thugs trips him and another kicks him, first in the head, then in the stomach. They all start hitting him with their fists. Someone finds a sturdy fallen branch and starts beating him senseless. One attacker smashes Dick in the head with a trash can while he is lying nearly unconscious on the sidewalk. Another pounds his head against the sidewalk, causing blood and brains to ooze over the cement. They continue beating him after his body is broken, bleeding, limp, and dead. They steal his boots and pull his jeans down to his knees. They cut off his genitals and stuff them in his mouth.

Luckily, Dick is not there to suffer this final inhumanity.

CHAPTER 12

Aftermath

June 1921

Most of the six thousand Blacks detained at the ballpark, Convention Hall, fairgrounds, and other camps are there for only three or four days. Others are held for weeks until a white man comes to vouch for them. Internees are forced to clean up the rubble that is now Greenwood without compensation and clean up camps that are barely more than wide-open spaces enclosed by tall walls.

Greenwood, the bustling Black Wall Street of North Tulsa, is incinerated. The Red Cross reports that nearly fifteen hundred homes and businesses are destroyed. Some three hundred homes are still standing but looted and badly damaged. Nearly forty blocks of a thriving African American community lie in ashes. Iron gates, brick chimneys, occasional outhouses, and columns of crumbling walls— formerly homes, churches, and businesses—jut out of the rubble as if to punctuate the carnage. The only building in the area not damaged or destroyed is Booker T. Washington High School on the northwest corner of Exeter Place and Haskell.

The Red Cross immediately sets up tents and food services for the homeless and interred, now including many of Greenwood's ten thousand Black citizens. The Salvation Army feeds thirty-seven Negro grave diggers on the first two days after the riot and twenty more the next day. There are no coffins, just Black bodies thrown into the graves and hastily covered over.

Black lawyers led by B. C. Franklin set up offices in tents to help process insurance claims for the victims, which proves to be a dishearteningly fruitless exercise. Later, Franklin is successful in getting a punitive fire ordinance declared unconstitutional. That ordinance makes it illegal to build in Greenwood with materials other than the very expensive stone and concrete, which effectively would have prohibited the Blacks from rebuilding.

So many prominent Black community leaders are dead or gone from Tulsa for good—the renowned, gentle surgeon Dr. A. C. Jackson, dead; Johnnie Johnson, owner of Johnson's fine men's clothing, shot while trying to protect his store; editors of both *The Oklahoma Sun* and *The Tulsa Star* shot, their newspapers burned to the ground; J. B. Stradford, entrepreneur and founder of the first luxury hotel for Blacks in Oklahoma, gone, never to return after being indicted for inciting the riot despite being already in police custody.

Ottawa W. Gurley—hotelier, entrepreneur, and father—is not indicted perhaps because he implicates other Black leaders, perhaps because he tries to facilitate the sale of Black property, or perhaps because he is one of the "reasonable Blacks" who argued against the march on the courthouse. Nevertheless, he soon leaves Tulsa and never returns.

Black families are separated and shattered, some never to be put back together again. Many flee the city, and many never return. Over sixty-five Black men are indicted. No white person is.

*****

The *Tulsa Tribune*'s blaming of the Blacks for the riot and the damage is relentless. Its position that the Blacks started the trouble and got what they deserved echoes the triumphant tone of many white Tulsans:

> ...a motley procession of Negroes...wended its way over the city's most prominent thorough-fares...to the ballpark. They held both hands above their heads, hat in one hand, as a symbol of their submission to the white man's authority...

They will return not to the homes they had on
Tuesday but to heaps of ashes, the angry white
man's reprisal for the wrong inflicted on them
by the inferior race... Tulsa Negroes had been
taught a lesson they would never forget, a lesson
for Negroes everywhere in America.

For several days, Black bodies still hang from trees or telephone poles or lie crumpled in streets, alleys, cars, and wagons. One
body is in a running pose, a man shot in the back without a chance.
Reminders of decimated families are everywhere: dropped dolls,
stuffed animals, scattered photographs, broken dishes, burned furnishings, a shoe here or there. Livestock still smolder in pens, fences
broken and burned. Shock and mourning comingle in a sour stew of
human suffering. The stench and misery are palpable.

Estimates of the dead are all over the board—from twenty-nine
dead Blacks and thirteen dead whites in official reports to more than
three hundred Blacks murdered according to eyewitness accounts.
There are reports of mass graves with scores of tangled Black bodies
dumped out of trucks and wagons. Bodies are charred beyond recognition, making accurate identification impossible in many cases.
Some believe the number of dead whites is underestimated so as not
to give credit to the Blacks for defending their property.

Adjutant general Charles Barrett, the head of the National
Guard, tours the area on June 3 and tells the press the following:

I have seen war zones and cities decimated
by war, but in all my years of military service,
I never saw a place so horrific. Schools and
churches, books, hymnals, and Bibles strewn over
the area beside smoldering buildings. Brick skele-
tons of buildings reduced to rubble and so many
homeless. Many in the nightclothes in which
they had fled, some with dead babies in their
arms Unsanitary conditions in makeshift tent
cities and in the detention camps run by the city.

An unintended consequence of the internment camps is a shortage of Black labor, which causes many white hotels and restaurants to shut down until white bosses can retrieve their employees. The vouchers save a lot of Blacks from much longer stays but also ensure that whites keep their cheap labor. When Blacks are released, they have to wear cards that read POLICE PROTECTION.

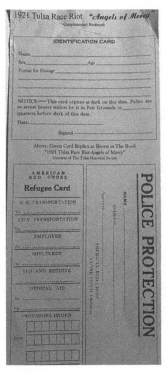

Police Protections Card required for Greenwood citizens
to wear on streets for months after Massacre
courtesy of the Tulsa Historical Society

*****

Immediately after the riot, promises are made. Alva J. Niles, president of the Tulsa Chamber of Commerce, says the city will care for its own: "Tulsa feels intensely humiliated...[by]...this great tragedy [and] pledges its every effort to wiping out the stain…and punishing those guilty of bringing the disgrace and disaster to this city."

None of these promises is kept, especially after the national newspapers tire of the story. And while the Chamber of Commerce tells the national press that reparation and restitution will be made, it is actually moving ahead with plans to build on the burned-out land, and city and civic leaders refuse assistance offered by outside agencies.

By the end of the day following the riot, the Real Estate Exchange begins urging Blacks to sell their land at the reduced new valuations. Richard Lloyd Jones of the *Tulsa Tribune* chimes in on June 4.

> The suggestion of the Real Estate Commission that the Negro district be moved out further, the burned-over area to be turned over to industry,… is a sensible one. If Tulsa business is to expand, the ground…now in ashes, is by all odds the most necessary to such expansion… Such a district as old Niggertown must never happen again.

Ottawa Gurley and Police Office Barney Cleaver work with white realtors to try to convince Black homeowners and business owners to sell. Due to the daunting task of rebuilding, many Blacks consider selling and moving farther north, but the Real Estate Exchange doesn't offer a fair price. Blacks want the value of the property prior to the massacre, but the Real Estate Exchange wants current market value. The insulting deal never gets done.

*****

On June 2, the probusiness *Tulsa World* runs an article that quotes former Mayor Loyal Martin near the end of the story: "Most of the looting and burning was done by white criminals who should have been shot." If anyone notices, they say nothing.

In a guest editorial for the *New York Post* on June 2, Richard Lloyd Jones reassures Eastern readers that there are "good Negros" in Tulsa, docile and respectful to whites, but also "bad Black men" who are beasts, dope fiends, bullies, and brutes. Thus, the *Tulsa Tribune* editor unabashedly mirrors the image of Gus, the rapacious Black man from *Birth of a Nation*, a very popular, racist 1915 movie screened at President Woodrow Wilson's White House.

Former President William Howard Taft writes in the *Washington Post* on June 6: "The awful character of this cruel massacre was largely due to the outrageous violence and cruelty of whites who took part in the conflict." For two weeks, the national and international press are all over the story, still calling it a Race Riot, though the only race that rioted were the whites who torched Black homes and businesses, sometimes with people inside.

*****

The story of Oklahoma is one of broken dreams and broken promises—from the Trail of Tears to the land rushes and to the Blacks and the poor whites, like Sarah Page, who dreamed of a better life. The stain and shame of these tragedies can never be erased.

The commerce, the vitality, of Greenwood has been vanquished, almost every block of the district a burned-out skeleton of what once was. But within days, homes and businesses are being reestablished in spite of ordinances forbidding it. White merchants are unwilling to redeem charred currency, and rebuilding is hard. Yet by Christmas, more than eight hundred frame houses and cement or brick build-ings have been constructed. This indomitable spirit epitomizes the pride, resilience, and entrepreneurial spirit of a community that will not be held down. Greenwood thrives until urban renewal and inte-gration finally break its back four decades later.

However, in June of 1921, this spirit seems to have collapsed—if only for the moment—under the weight of the Memorial Day catastrophe. The nearly hopeless meander aimlessly or languish in long soup lines, mingling with broken bodies and decimated dreams.

CHAPTER 13

A Day of Reckoning?

2000–2001

"Well, Don is as good as his word. This is his commission. Let's see what they do," Hattie says to Lucy as they take their seats for the hearing. "But I did think there would be a bill introduced to ask for reparations."

"No. Remember, he said the only way these crackers would give up any of their money, especially to Blacks, is if a study is done first based on depositions and public hearings, so we have to be patient. You know the government—glaciers move faster. I have confidence in Don. You taught him well."

Oklahoma State Representative Don Ross, along with legislative aide Wilbur McNeely, had recruited Hattie and Lucy three years ago to help conduct interviews and collect depositions for the hearings. As she waits for the proceedings to start, Hattie remembers what Wilbur had told them in the fall of 1997:

> The goal of the Commission and Report is to hold public hearings and invite the media so everyone knows what's going on and what went on all those years ago. Our report and the hearings must clearly lay out what happened. Just be aware, ladies, some folks will not believe the truth.

A hush falls over the gallery as Rep. Ross takes the floor and, after some preliminaries, asks one survivor after another to tell his or her personal story of the horrors that took place on May 31 and June 1, 1921. "I wonder if you would mind telling us a little about the events you saw or heard going on around town in Tulsa or Greenwood that night or the next morning," he coaxes. "If you need to stop and gather your composure, please do so." Along with Lucy and others in the gallery, Hattie listens with rapt attention as Don introduces each witness in turn.

*****

Veneice Sims, aged ninety-four, who was a teenager at the time of the riot:

> It was a terrible thing. I had been to Mabel's beauty shop because our Washington High School Junior-Senior Prom was that night. We were having the prom at the fancy new Stradford Hotel, and we were all excited. It was to be my first prom. Blue is my favorite color, and I had laid my peacock-blue sateen dress there on the bed just so with the matching blue shoes and a pearl necklace I had borrowed from Mrs. White, the seamstress who made my dress. I loved that dress. I never saw it again.
>
> We never had a prom. They burned down the Stradford Hotel, and I never saw my boyfriend again either. I heard that he and his family fled to Detroit during the days immediately after the riot. That's what happened. Some folks walked to safe places, up to sixty miles on foot. Others hopped on freight trains and left the state. Some piled into wagons drawn by mules or horses as far as they could go. Some were put in the camps. Some came back to find their homes

or businesses in ruins. Others were never heard from again, and I believe in my heart that they perished in that riot.

George Jackson, son of respected surgeon Dr. A. C. Jackson, who was shot and killed in the early morning hours of June 1:

> I was six years old. When the white men came into our house, my sister Beulah grabbed me and my three brothers and pulled us under the bed in our parents' bedroom. I was plenty scared, but Beulah kept me quiet until we thought the men were gone. Then we ran out the back door and found Momma hiding in the bushes, and the six of us headed north looking for our daddy, but he never came home from his house call.

Julius Scott, whose parents told him about their flight from Greenwood on the morning of June 1:

> My mother and father were sitting in the living room of our house on Easton, between Greenwood and Hartford. A man ran in and said a riot was on, and they started walking. Momma was pregnant with me, her second child, and a man came along in a Model T and gave my family a ride to a stop on the Sand Springs Streetcar Line at Pine. Momma said she saw a truckload of men who had painted their arms and faces black. Airplanes flew over low and dropped a bomb that hit the truck and killed many of those men.

Eunice Cummings, daughter of a courageous father who died protecting his family:

> Our daddy went out with a gun and said he was goin' to the courthouse because Dick Rowland was about to be lynched by the Ku Klux Klan. My momma begged him not to go, but he went anyway. He came back late that night and was bleeding. He said, "We stopped 'em at the Frisco tracks. They didn't come into Greenwood." But lots of our neighbors were pilin' stuff into their cars and leavin' town. Momma told Daddy we should leave, but he said, "This is my home. They'll have to kill me first." We left, but Daddy didn't, and they burned our house down with him in it.

Mabel Black, who, along with her husband, ran several successful businesses in Greenwood:

> We had four rental houses, all paid for. I had a beauty salon—a real good business too—and Alva had his café. Everyone went there at least once a week to see or be seen. The sight of everything we worked so hard for reduced to ashes nearly killed my Alva, but he went right to work. He was a model of discipline and sacrifice. We completed the new beauty salon just before he died.
>
> He caught tuberculosis, but that riot killed my Alva just as sure as if they'd shot him dead like they did so many. He worked like a mule cleaning up the mess they made of everything, and he built us a new home in spite of all the laws made to stop us.

Justin Brown, who, along with the rest of his family, ran for his life on June 1:

> I was ten years old, and my big brother was supposed to go to that prom. I found out later that the hotel had burned down in the troubles, but he sure was mad that night. Had a date with a real good-looking gal too.
>
> The next morning, we thought the troubles of the night before were over. We had not heard about all of the terrible things that happened because we didn't live that close to Greenwood Avenue or Archer. So because we thought it was safe, my brothers and sisters and I were playing in our front yard. Then we heard a whistle or a siren or something, and soon enough, bullets started dropping into our yard. They looked like little black birds. I didn't know if I should drop to the ground or run for the house.
>
> My father heard the bullets hitting the roof and the side of the house. He came running out into the yard and gathered us up into the house right quick. Then he decided the mob was getting too close and that we better run for safety. As we ran along a little farther, we could see cars full of white men driving down Greenwood Avenue, guns blazing and bullets flying at Black people—men, women, and children—running north.
>
> My father's boss, a white man named Sandy McDonald, saved our lives that day. Papa was well-known as the best mechanic in Tulsa, Black or white, and Mr. McDonald owned a garage in Greenwood and one in South Tulsa. Daddy worked at both.
>
> We were running from the mobsters, scared out of our wits. Then who should we see but

Mr. McDonald. He came to rescue us. We piled into the back seat of his black Franklin car, and he took us to his home in South Tulsa. It was a nice house, and he and his wife kept us and fed us until it was safe to return to Greenwood. We could see Greenwood burning from his front porch. It was a pitiful sight.

Calvin Gibbs, grandson of a prominent hotelier in Greenwood:

My grandfather was Otis Gibbs. He did his best to protect his property, the Red Wing Hotel, that night and the next morning, but he was overcome by smoke from his own hotel, so he ran down the back stairs and headed north. He made it as far as Easton Street where a few armed, drunk teenagers had corralled about fifty Negro men, women, and children, all with their hands in the air. After being searched and beaten by his captors, he was pushed into line with the rest of the Blacks and marched up Greenwood Avenue to the detention center at Convention Hall.

There, women were forced to hand over their purses and any jewelry, including wedding rings. The men were forced to empty their pockets and then were pushed into the large hall with the barrels and butts of shotguns and rifles. One man was shot at the convention center after he had surrendered.

Harriet Thomas, descendant of a family subjected to an unimaginable cruelty:

My great aunt was Callie Rodgers. She had a very sick daughter and couldn't leave the house. But a couple of white men yanked her out into the street, strapped her tightly to a chair, and set her house on fire with her six-year-old daughter inside as she watched helplessly. She found the charred body of her little girl the next afternoon and never got over it.

Harry Richardson, whose uncle witnessed terrible atrocities:

Uncle Thaddeus told me he saw this white fellow dressed in a cowboy outfit wielding a long bullwhip. That cowboy took special delight in lassoing the ankles of young children. My uncle saw him tangle up one young girl and flip her in front of a horse-drawn wagon, which crushed her. He caught a little boy and threw him right under the four giant bay horses that were galloping through the streets. Another young boy was torn to pieces, and his parents had to keep running for fear the rest of their children would be killed as well.

And finally, a middle-aged woman who lost her relatives in horrific fashion:

Three thugs grabbed my grandparents, Mildred and Wes Watson, who were in their seventies, and pushed them into the street in their nightclothes and shot them in front of their home with their hands up.

*****

"Horrible, horrible," Rep. Ross says, dabbing his eye with a large fuchsia handkerchief as the granddaughter of the Watsons leaves the stand. "Ladies and gentlemen of the Commission, I suggest that we break for the week before we move on to hear testimony from people who dispute the previous testimony."

Hattie and Lucy wait for Rep. Ross just outside the hearing room door, catching him before he rushes off to another meeting. "I know who you are going to call to the stand next week, Don, but I don't understand why," a bewildered Lucy remarks.

"I just don't see any way around it, Attorney Barnes. These people are repositories of Tulsa history—"

"And a repository of Tulsa hatred."

"I just don't think these hearings will have any credibility if we don't hear from the other side, and I believe their bias will speak for itself. Besides, none of them is an eyewitness or the descendant of people there that day."

"Give voice to the devil himself if you like," Lucy retorts, "but you'll understand if I am not in the room."

"I'd join you if I could."

*****

The following week, the hearings resume. The first person to testify is Beryl Ford, an older white man who teeters to the stand with the help of a metal walker. He was not born until 1926 but credits his superior knowledge of Tulsa Negroes and the Race Riot of 1921 to his sixty-year membership in the Tulsa Pioneers, who annually tell their version of the story. A structural engineer, Ford had worked in a mortuary in Wichita, Kansas, before coming to Tulsa.

"The Negroes at the Tulsa County Courthouse were drunk thugs," he testifies, "not World War I veterans. The whites were curiosity seekers who came to the courthouse because they heard that the Negroes were going to storm the jail where Dick Rowland was being held under extreme security."

Ford claims there weren't enough trucks to carry three hundred dead bodies to mass graves and that if they had been dumped in the river, they would have popped up somewhere. He also remarks that no one who testified last week mentioned the smell: "The stench of dead bodies is strong and bitter as hell. If that many bodies had been stacked up anywhere, there'd have been a terrible stink."

"Let the record show that Mr. Ford had worked in a mortuary, shaving and embalming bodies, before moving to Tulsa in the 1940s," Rep. Ross interjects.

Ford further states that the six airplanes were only there to protect the Blacks. "The old airplanes were made of canvass," he adds, "and no one in their right mind would light an incendiary device in an open canvass plane." When he leaves the stand at the conclusion of his testimony, people in the audience can be heard talking among themselves and refuting his statements.

"You're a liar and a racist," a Black man yells.

"You are too," Ford yells back.

His testimony is followed by that of another white man who, like Ford, had not yet been born or had relatives in Tulsa at the time of the riots. "The Negroes were better off in the detention camps than they had been before the riot," Bill O'Brien testifies. "They had running water and hot showers. The Red Cross and many ladies from white churches prepared three meals a day for those interned, and supper was always a hot meal. There were even laundry facilities nearby they could go out to and use."

"It wouldn't have mattered if it were the Taj Mahal," a Black lady in the audience interrupts. "They were held there without their consent and with no charges filed against them, and they had to wait for a white person to come to vouch for them before they could get out." Rep. Ross raises his hand to bring the woman to order despite his seeming reluctance to do so.

*****

Behind closed doors, the commissioners are concerned. "Reparation costs for property damage alone could run into the millions. We can't pay out that kind of money for something our ancestors maybe did or maybe did not," one commissioner complains.

There are two legislators on the Commission, Senator Robert Milacek of Waukomis and Representative Abe Deutschendorf (uncle of singer John Denver) of Lawton. They both are opposed to reparations paid by the state. "If this is presented to the legislature, it is unlikely to get much support," Sen. Milacek tells the other commissioners. "People are going to say, 'If we do this for Tulsa, where does it stop—Mennonites whose homes were burned during World War I, American Indians?' We could go on forever."

Rep. Deutschendorf says the state does not have any responsibility for the riot. "You did not make any argument convincing to me, and I would not be able to make that argument to my colleagues."

It seems the commissioners all have reached the same tacit conclusion: "Taxpayers will never agree to this."

*****

In February 2001, the report from the Oklahoma Commission to Study the Tulsa Race Riot of 1921 finally comes out. Hattie and Lucy watch the announcement on TV. Governor Frank Keating says he has always favored reparations "if you can show liability on behalf of the state." Tulsa Mayor Susan Savage says she favors reparations but does not offer any city funds.

Talking to reporters afterward, Rep. Ross appears incensed: "A mob torched the soul of the city, an evil from which neither Blacks nor whites have fully recovered, and nothing is done about it. Where is justice, and why is it being denied to these American citizens?"

"Well, like Uncle Hiram told Aunt Damie, 'Don't expect nuthin' and you won't be disappointed,'" Hattie says to Lucy, shaking her head.

Six months later, Senate Bill 234, the Tulsa Race Riot Reconciliation Bill, meets with a fate similar to that of the Commission and Report and for similar reasons. Again, little is accomplished. But Rep. Ross is neither surprised nor discouraged. Rather, he simply asks himself, "What now?"

CHAPTER 14

What Now?

2001

After a toothless bill with no reparations, scholarships, memorials, or anything meaningful is signed by Gov. Frank Keating, Hattie complains bitterly to Lucy. "Look what they did for the Japanese, for Rosewood, the Holocaust survivors. Hell, even the Indians got forty acres and a mule."

"But not for us, girlfriend, not for us," Lucy replies, outraged, "not a dime. And to add insult to injury, the state is giving each survivor or descendant a gold-plated medal with the Oklahoma state seal. Can you believe it?"

Hattie doesn't even try to hide her disappointment. Both she and Lucy had figured the legislature would do something. Still seething, Hattie answers the phone with a brisk hello. On the other end of the line, Rep. Ross asks, "Are you ready?"

"Ready? Seems like it's all over to me, Don."

"Naw, naw, Miss Hattie. We have not yet begun to fight. Wilbur will be in our Tulsa office on Thursday, and he wants to introduce you and Attorney Barnes to the new lead on the case. He's a firecracker, not a white cracker."

"What do you want us to meet with him for? What can we do?"

"No one expects you to physically do a lot," Don quickly reassures. "What we want is your advice and counsel, and we want you to advise the team of lawyers conducting the final depositions. I know you have read all the survivors' interviews and the report from the Commission. Now we need to start putting all that into court exhibits and get usable depositions. We're off to the appellate court, and you and Attorney Barnes know there will be no money coming for anything to do with the riot unless the court orders it."

*****

Thursday morning, Hattie and Lucy both happen to be attired in brightly colored sundresses with short-sleeved jackets as they make the short trip to Don's Tulsa office. Legislative aide Wilbur McNeely greets the two women warmly and ushers them into a conference room.

Before excusing himself to attend to other business, Wilbur introduces Charlie Crabtree, a tall, elegant Black lawyer nattily dressed in a classic black suit with a chartreuse handkerchief square that matches his skinny tie. He's wearing shiny black Italian leather shoes. After kissing each woman's hand in turn, he proclaims that absolutely perfect groundwork has been laid—by him—to prepare a case to be filed in the Tenth District Court of Appeals. "Now we just need to get our proverbial ducks in a row," he explains.

He will be the lead attorney on the case, doing his work pro bono, along with several lawyers from the original dream team that has worked together since before the Commission hearings. Crabtree tells the ladies that the strategies will be similar to those used for the Commission. "We could expect a decision whether or not to hear the case in the next twenty-four months. But I have to ask you ladies, why? This seems so very personal to you. You weren't even born at the time of the riots, Attorney Barnes. And you, Miss Hattie, you were born in Kansas City."

Hattie feels herself wince at the mention of Kansas City where she lived so long and so happily with her mother. Even though later difficulties meant they had to leave Kansas, she still misses those times almost every day of her life. She haltingly begins to tell her story.

*****

"I never knew my father. He was Dick Rowland. My mother was Sarah Page. He died before I was born, and I was raised by my mother and Dick's aunt Damie in the home of a very gracious and generous white couple who were his friends. Aunt Damie and Momma and I were so happy at the Adams—that is, until the Depression and the black blizzard forced us to leave. Momma had to go back to her people in Sand Springs. She couldn't take a Black child home, so I went to Tulsa with Aunt Damie. It was wretched. I was almost a teenager. I was being separated from my mother."

After a few deep breaths, Hattie gathers her thoughts and continues. "Momma and Aunt Damie saved every penny, even during the Depression, and I worked several jobs too. Because of the horrible dust storms, I couldn't even go to high school for two years, so we all worked and saved to make sure I could get an education.

"I saw Momma some during that time, but it was hard. She worked seven days a week when she could, and she had to catch a ride in from Sand Springs and back because the public transportation was so unreliable. She was afraid to use it in case she couldn't get back in time for work. She would have been fired, even from her uncle's grocery store, one of the three jobs she had. It wasn't safe for me to go there.

"Although everyone bragged how Black Wall Street had risen from the ashes of the terrible fires, it didn't much matter because we didn't have any extra money to buy things. Besides, by the time we got there, the stores that had been rebuilt were ravaged by the Depression and the dust, and many were just boarded up and empty.

"No one ever spoke of the race riot, though they did mention that much of Greenwood had burned down before I was born. Massive, destructive fires were not uncommon at that time, so I wasn't curious at first. I didn't find out about what caused the burning for years, after I finally nagged Momma into telling me about my daddy."

Hattie glances quickly toward Lucy, who nods her support. "I badgered her so much for so long that one day, when I had just started high school, she relented and told me the whole ugly story, told me about how they sparked the riot. Her guilt and shame were palpable. I felt sorry for her and angry at the same time. I couldn't really blame her or my daddy. They were just stupid teenagers in love, and Momma was pregnant with me.

"She and Aunt Damie kept this secret from me for more than sixteen years. I resented it at first, but not after I understood the toll it had taken on them. What I didn't understand was why no one in Greenwood ever talked about the riot. Aunt Damie said people were afraid it might happen again if they talked about it, and I knew Momma and Aunt Damie didn't want anyone in Greenwood to find out my real identity.

"So now I had this huge secret and conflicting feelings—I suppose like a lot of teenagers. But it still tore me apart each time I separated from Momma and to never have met my daddy. Even after I learned the awful truth, Aunt Damie told me wonderful stories about him as a boy. But I missed my momma. I missed Kansas City. I was forlorn, and my heart was so, so very heavy." Holding back her own tears, Hattie sees that Lucy's eyes are red, and her cheeks are wet.

*****

Lucy is grateful she isn't asked to weigh in during Hattie's story. Reparations and other compensations are important to her for all the reasons that the destruction of one's community would be important to anyone with a conscience. But it is personal to her because it's personal to Hattie. They grew up together, married and raised their kids together, buried their husbands and mothers together. She knows how this has hung over Hattie like a noose waiting to choke her, an ugly albatross hovering overhead her whole life.

Lucy remembers that day after school—she and Hattie had known each other only a few weeks but liked each other immediately—when her new friend started talking about the riot. Lucy's mother had never told her about white people torturing and murdering Negroes in Greenwood and burning the whole district to the ground not even twenty years earlier. Greenwood was better and safer than Oklahoma City during the Depression, her mother always said.

Once Lucy learned the truth about the riots and her new friend's terrible secret, the girls became inextricably bonded.

*****

Atty. Crabtree is moved and visibly shaken by what he has heard. "I promise you, Miss Hattie, we will do everything we can to redress as many of the grievances perpetrated on Tulsa's Black community as we can. I know we cannot repair the aching hole in your heart, but I hope we can take a step toward mending this community that was ripped apart by so many atrocities so many years ago."

CHAPTER 15

Goin' to Kansas City

June–December 1921

Getting out of Greenwood is treacherous. Police, National Guard, and marauding mobs of drunk vigilantes still patrol the smoldering streets. Jimmy holds his breath almost until they are safely out of town. He breathes a little easier once they reach the Kansas state line. He can tell Damie and Sarah are just as scared and heartbroken by the carnage as he is.

The trip to Kansas City is long. Although it's only two hundred miles or so, the roads are not great, and it's dark for most of the first part of the trip when the ladies should be sleeping but apparently cannot. Jimmy hears Damie humming a low, slow, sad gospel tune, followed by a softly whispered prayer: "Dear Lord, please keep my boy Dick safe from harm. Deliver him from evil. Oh Lord, my sweet Lord, please bring Dick back to us. And please, Lord, accept the soul of your faithful servant Uncle Hiram into your kingdom. He deserves a rest from the trials this here earth has put him through."

Jimmy had put Sarah in the front seat and Damie in the back. He hopes the older lady can get some rest, but mostly, he wants a white face in the front seat if anyone looks in, especially the police. He knows there are some pretty ornery sheriffs in these parts. Under other circumstances, he and his passengers might be singing or at least chatting, maybe laughing. But this night, after what they've seen and heard, there is no laughter, there is no conversation, there are no words.

Jimmy has tried to be kind and positive. He didn't ask about Dick when he picked up the two women at Greenwood and Archer. Sarah said he would be along directly, and he left it at that. He assumes the worst about Dick but keeps it to himself.

He and Dick have been friends for years—played football together, dropped out of high school together, made money shining shoes together. Jimmy has a second job at Williams Garage, but Dick stayed shining shoes for the tips. They hung out together a lot at the County Line, and he knows Sarah from there.

Fortunately, one of the cars at Williams Garage wasn't destroyed. Mr. Williams had left town by train, and his wife loaned the car to Jimmy to help Dick and Sarah get away. Mrs. Williams is staying on the edge of town with relatives, and Jimmy plans to drop off the car when he returns so she and their children can join Mr. Williams in Illinois.

Jimmy stops the green Model T when it's safe. Some places, he can fill the tank, maybe buy a soda or sandwich or use the usually disgusting Coloreds-only restroom. Earlier, he had packed blankets, food and water, and a five-gallon can of gasoline because he knows most places on their route will not serve Negroes. Jimmy has his own silent prayer: "Sweet Jesus, don't let us get stopped by no cops. Don't let this car break down. Please keep us safe."

*****

Throughout the night and into the next day, Sarah worries terribly that something will happen or has happened to Dick. "I hope those boys didn't hurt him none," she says to herself. "I should of gone back or got help. I sure hope he's all right."

She thinks about when she first met Dick at the County Line. It took her breath away watching him dance. He was the only man who ever bought her a drink. She remembers how he was all excited about her being from Sand Springs. He had asked if she had ever seen Bill Pickett, the Black cowboy who started something called bulldogging.

She didn't know what the hell bulldogging was but pretended to be interested just to keep Dick talking in that beautiful, velvety voice. It felt like a gentle caress when he spoke. "If I ever prayed, I'd be prayin' like hell now," Sarah tells herself. "No matter, I plan on cuttin' a rug with that boy before I get too big to dance."

She and Damie had met only briefly once before. They do not know each other at all, and she suspects neither thinks highly of the other. But she also knows they are united in their fear. Mostly, they are just plain worried about Dick.

Toward the end of their journey, Sarah feels she should tell her two companions her secret and see what they think about when and how to tell the Adams but she can't find the words.

*****

It is about noon the next day when they finally arrive in Kansas City where Jean and Henry Adams are welcoming. They had known Damie and Dick years ago in Tulsa before they moved to Kansas. "Where's Rowland?" Henry asks immediately. News of the Negro uprising had hit the Kansas City papers, but he discreetly does not mention it, fearing Dick may be one of the casualties.

"He should be 'long directly," Damie answers. "Had a few loose ends to tie up."

"Well, he's one smart fellow. I'm sure he'll figure it out," he says hopefully.

Henry is a bookish man with short, thin reddish-blond hair and thick black glasses that mostly hide his hazel eyes. In his late thirties, Henry already has a stocky frame. He grew up on a farm in West Kansas with his younger brother and two sisters, then went to Tulsa to try to cash in on the oil boom. That was where he met his wife, Jean, who grew up in Tahlequah but had come to the big city to make her fortune as a secretary. They met at church and married soon afterward.

Jean's aunt had taken them in that first year, which was when they met Dick Rowland, though not at church. Damie worked for friends of Jean's aunt, and the couple fell in love with the spunky youngster almost immediately. They watched him head off to high school football fame before they left for Kansas to be closer to Henry's family.

Jean was the only child of elderly parents, and they had given her their blessing to go make a life for herself in Tulsa. She is a few years younger than Henry. Today, she is modestly dressed in a brightly colored gingham housedress, peach and blue with orange checks and a white Peter Pan collar. The dress has large patch pockets, which mostly cannot be seen because she is wearing a long apron, also with practical large pockets.

Jean is not homely but not terribly pretty. She has a round face and a turned-up nose with freckles across its bridge. She has gorgeous auburn hair with light waves, which she wears loosely to her shoulders, and deep-blue eyes. Most winningly, she has a warm, infectious laugh that rumbles from deep within.

Henry had come home for lunch hoping to welcome Dick, Jimmy, and the two women to Kansas City. Hanging in the hallway are his straw hat and a slim-fitting dark-brown suit jacket, which, now removed, exposes a matching vest, the type of attire worn by most of the men at the bank.

As he greets Damie, he reminds her how Dick, even as a youngster, always took extra special care with his clothing and grooming. "He was a good-looking little fellow," Henry says. "Always on the move, like he had ants in his pants."

"He was just dancin'," Damie responds. "He loved the jazz and blues, always dancin'." And now she silently prays he's not dancing at the end of a rope—or worse.

"For tonight, we'll put you and Sarah in the garage apartment out back. It's not much, but there's a hot plate and a small refrigerator and a cot and bed. Kind of crowded. And, Jimmy, if you don't mind, you can bunk on a cot in the storage room—what should be a spare bedroom."

"Thanks, Mr. Adams, but I gotta be startin' back. My boss's wife will need this here car."

"Well, at least get a couple of hours of shut-eye before you make that drive again. Mrs. Adams will pack you a lunch for the trip back."

"This is so nice of y'all," Damie says. "Cain't thank you enough for lettin' us stay and work here."

"When Rowland gets here, we will find another spot for you, Damie. We can fix up that spare room."

"Anythin' is fine by me, honest. We're just grateful to be here, and we pray Dick will git here soon." Sarah had told her briefly of the scuffle, but she has put it out of her mind. Neither woman mentions it to the Adams.

*****

Damie misses Tulsa and the Greenwood she had known, but she and Sarah rarely talk about it. The women have fallen into an amicable working arrangement, not yet warm but becoming less distant, Damie believes. Once she was able to make contact, Damie told a few relatives in Tulsa that she's in Kansas City, but she does not tell whom she's with or with whom she's staying. Now she anxiously awaits letters from Tulsa and reports to Sarah what she learns.

Dick still does not come. After several weeks, a letter from Tulsa tells Damie that Dick was murdered while they were making their getaway. Upon hearing the terrible news, Sarah blurts out, "I'm gonna have Dick's baby, and he ain't never gonna meet his daddy." She runs sobbing from the room.

Damie had suspected as much but said nothing. Now she and Jean stare at each other. "I promise you, we will do everything we can for Sarah and the baby, Dick's baby," Jean says. "Do you think you should speak to her, tell her we're here for her?" Damie nods and goes to their apartment.

"Now, Chile, we all loved Dick. He was a lovable cuss. But now we gots to focus on your baby. Mrs. Adams say they'll do everythin' they can to help, and you know I will. We'll get through this, girl. I promise."

"Oh, Aunt Damie, why didn't I go back to help Dick or run for help? I didn't do nuthin', and now he's dead."

"You know there wasn't nuthin' you coulda done, Sarah. Them boys woulda kilt you too, maybe raped you. You'd a lost your baby,

Dick's baby. That's what we gotta think 'bout now. And I'll be prayin' for Dick's soul."

Jean tells Henry about Dick when he gets home from work. The household is unanimous in their grief. Few words are spoken, but a sour shroud of sadness swallows them up for the rest of the summer.

*****

July is brutally hot, and the ladies rest at midday even before Sarah starts showing. Sarah and Damie work side by side at the Adams modest but comfortable one-story house. Damie also takes in ironing. The home has an open porch across the front of the house with a porch swing that fills almost the entire west end of the porch. The house is on a corner lot with cherry laurel bushes enclosing the side yard, large oak trees in front, and a crepe myrtle in the back between the main house and the garage apartment where Sarah and Damie stay.

Henry works weekdays downtown at the bank. He's called a manager, but he's actually little more than a teller and not high enough in management to help Sarah get an elevator job in the building. Quite the gardener, he grows vegetables and roses all summer long in the patch of ground between the main house and the garage apartment.

Damie cooks up fresh vegetables every night and bakes bread once a week. Jean fixes chicken or meat loaf and potatoes most nights, and the four of them eat dinner together in the dining room, which looks out on the side yard. Sarah and Damie clean and, with Jean's help, do the laundry, hang it out to dry, fold it, and put it away. In addition to room and board, the two ladies receive a modest stipend they could use on a movie or a meal but instead save, along with the ironing money, for the future of Sarah and Dick's baby.

Sarah grows bigger month by month and gets some gentle ribbing from Damie and Jean. She's a sturdy girl and continues to work almost up to Christmas, when the baby is due. Henry and Jean have never had children of their own, and they grow more excited each day about Sarah's baby. They are even more excited about the upcoming birth than about Christmas, which has always been their favorite time of year.

Every year, including this one, they start decorating immediately after Thanksgiving with a large fir tree Henry buys at City Market on Fourth Street and Walnut, not far from the bank. Although she's big as a house, Sarah tries to get in the holiday spirit by helping with the decorations.

When Sarah goes into labor a few days before Christmas, Jean starts boiling water, ripping up old sheets, and grabbing clean towels and alcohol. Earlier, she had moved Sarah inside the house, to the small spare bedroom, replacing the cot with a twin bed in anticipation. Not much more than a broom closet, the room would have been a nursery for an Adams offspring had the opportunity presented itself.

Damie, who had delivered many Negro babies, prepares to deliver the child. She boils a sharp kitchen knife to cut the umbilical cord, and Sarah does her best to contain her screams. The beautiful baby is delivered without incident. All three women, who took part in the delivery, beam with joy and pride.

They had called for the doctor knowing he would not arrive by the time the baby was delivered. When he arrives and sees it is a Negro baby, he perfunctorily signs the birth certificate, not paying any attention to names. He gets the race right and does not ask the father's name. The white doctor would not have come, Jean knew, if the house had been in the Colored section. Damie handles all the interaction with the doctor, purposely not giving either Dick's or Sarah's real name in order to protect the child in the future. Fortunately, Henry is at work, because he can be a bit of a stickler about rules.

Months earlier, Sarah had inquired about a photograph of Jean's beloved aunt who had taken in Jean and Henry when they were getting started. Before the birth, Sarah told Damie, "If this baby is a girl, I'm going to name her Hattie in honor of the matriarch of this family who have so kindly taken us in. If it's a boy, I'll name him Hiram."

Hattie Mae Johnson fills the household with genuine Christmas cheer.

CHAPTER 16

Mostly Happy Days

1922–1929

The Kansas economy is booming in the 1920s. Though strictly segregated, Blacks in both Kansas City, Kansas, and Kansas City, Missouri, are doing pretty well. Jazz is making its way into popular culture, and Black musicians flock to both cities to partake of the surge in the popularity of their sound. Modern skyscrapers dot the landscape, and cable cars shuttle people around their vibrant communities.

Territorial Kansas had been an abolitionist stronghold. It was not a slave state and had become an important stop on Harriet Tubman's Underground Railroad. However, many of its early settlers were from the South and brought their racial prejudices with them. There are bombings of Negro housing in the 1920s in the historic Quindaro district of Kansas City, Kansas, at the convergence of the Kansas and Missouri Rivers. But in spite of mutual suspicion, the races exist separately and peacefully for the most part.

The earliest college for Coloreds west of the Mississippi River— Quindaro Freedman's School (later Western University)—was chartered in Kansas City, Kansas, in 1865. Across the Missouri River, the other Kansas City boasts the Blues stadium for the Negro National League. In 1925, the all-Black Wichita Monrovian baseball team beats the KKK team 10–8. By the end of the 1920s, there are twenty-six Black schools and thirty-eight Black churches in the Kansas City area.

*****

Hattie Mae Johnson is christened at the Second Baptist Church near Eighteenth Street and Vine in Kansas City, Kansas. It's not the closest church to where her family lives, but it is a Negro church that will baptize a Black baby even if she's brought in by one Colored (Damie) and three whites (Sarah, Jean, and Henry) and causes some eyebrows to be raised when passersby observe the scene. Damie plays the piano at Second Baptist, and when she's a little older, Hattie sits in the choir loft with her.

Sarah works the Sunday church shift at the diner. She almost never goes to church in Kansas City. She tells Damie that people stare at her funny at the Black church, and if she does decide to go to church, it will be with her daughter. She can't take Hattie to a white church, so she works most every Sunday.

Sarah and Hattie move into the garage apartment in the back, and Damie moves into the spare room inside the house. After Sarah gets a job, Damie spends a lot of time with Hattie. She cherishes her time with the blossoming baby girl.

Sarah's job as a waitress allows her to pay the Adams a bit of rent. Sometimes, she can bring diner food home for the family. She makes pretty good money, especially the tips. Damie continues working for the Adams, taking in ironing and watching Hattie with care and pride. Sarah works the lunch shift or, sometimes, breakfast at the diner so she can be home when Hattie gets out of school.

Under other circumstances, Sarah tells Damie, she might like to taste the nightlife on Eighteenth and Vine. Sometimes, it seems she can hardly breathe for the weight of the aching pain of her guilt over what happened to Dick and the whole Tulsa disaster. Damie can see that Sarah is engulfed in an enervating fog penetrated only by the light that is Hattie. She knows Sarah silently cries herself to sleep when she can sleep at all. Damie feels helpless, but Sarah always gathers herself by morning.

Letters from friends and relatives in Tulsa tell Damie about how quickly Greenwood is recovering. "Not yet the former Black Wall Street but a bustling, thriving community once again," a friend writes to her early in 1924. She usually tells Sarah any interesting news, but they have very few shared memories of that time—Sarah was mostly in white Tulsa, and Damie was in Greenwood.

*****

Country Club Plaza, the first planned suburban shopping center in the world, opened in Kansas City, Missouri, in 1923. Designed in the Moorish Revival style, the Plaza was an instant success, at least in part because its multilevel parking accommodated visitors arriving by automobile. On her fourth birthday, Hattie, along with Sarah and Damie, pile into the back seat of the Adams's Buick to see the Plaza's incredible display of colored Christmas lights in 1925, the same year she enters kindergarten.

Henry and Jean Adams couldn't love little Hattie more if she were their own. She is smart and curious and thirsty for learning even before she can get into school. Once she starts kindergarten at White Church Elementary School—on the second floor because the first floor is for white children—she excels. Hattie doesn't care where she goes to school. She is learning, and she is exhilarated.

When Hattie gets old enough, she helps Damie with the housework and joins Henry in the garden. However, her homework is always the number one priority for everyone. Afternoon rituals include the ladies playing word games with Hattie and helping her with her homework, which she increasingly insists she doesn't need. In the summer, Hattie uses the front porch swing as her pirate ship and Jean's yardstick as a sword. Sometimes, on a Saturday afternoon when Sarah is working, Damie and Hattie make chocolate chip cookies for everyone to enjoy for dessert that night and the next day at Sunday supper.

There's a new amusement park in town, but Blacks are not allowed, and Sarah cannot bring herself to go. Damie and the Adams encourage her to get out a little, but they do not press. They all can see she is suffering under a brave face. If she doesn't have to work, Sarah will sometimes go with Hattie and Damie to Negro day at the zoo, a monthly ritual since Hattie was four.

It's a good zoo, and Hattie is fascinated with the animals. Her eyes pop at the sheer size of the elephants, the long necks of the giraffes, and the striped horses. She laughs out loud at the antics of the chimpanzees, and is mesmerized by the majesty of the lions—the King of the Beasts, Damie tells her. Hattie is intrigued by the way the big cats rub each other's noses and faces, which she says reminds her of when her momma gives her "Eskimo kisses." At first, she doesn't understand how that can be since Eskimos live where it is cold, not in Africa. Later, she learns that the Sahara Desert, near where the lions live, is the largest hot desert in the world. Not knowing there was such a thing as a cold desert, she reads about it as much as she can.

When she gets a bit older, about six, Damie tells her during one of their zoo visits that her favorite animals are from Africa, which is full of Colored people and where all Blacks in America come from. She has to know more both about Africa and the animals. She is particularly interested in the lions. There are maps at the zoo, but Hattie is uncertain as to exactly where Africa is.

That week, Hattie goes down to the public library after school. Since Coloreds are not allowed, she waits in the delivery bay until someone tells the kindly librarian she is there. Mrs. Harris usually brings Hattie books she thinks are appropriate, and she has learned that Hattie always returns them within a week in the same condition or better than she found them. Hattie has made new covers for several books since she started borrowing them from the library.

Today, Hattie asks the librarian if she can have any books on Africa and the animals at the zoo, especially the lion. Mrs. Harris is a little surprised but promises she'll have the books for her next week. She quickly gives Hattie the three books she had already selected for her so she can get back to work before her absence is noticed.

The next week, Mrs. Harris has four books for Hattie. She learns where Africa is and that Blacks were royalty and well-educated people before being brought to the Americas as slaves and forced to perform hard, unpaid labor. She had heard a little bit about slavery, and these books didn't tell her too much more but certainly more than she knew. Every week, she gets more books, mostly about Africa, to the obvious delight of Mrs. Harris.

Hattie learns that the lion is one of the most social of the cats, living in groups called "prides" that consist of a few adult males, more adult females, and lots of cubs. She reads that they live in grasslands and savannas mostly in sub-Saharan Africa. Sub-Saharan Africa is near the equator, which divides the earth between the Northern and Southern hemispheres. She certainly wants to know more about all of that.

As her reading progresses, she is fascinated to learn that lions weigh about three pounds when they are born and cannot see until they are about three weeks old. By the time that they are a year old, they weigh about fifty pounds, almost as much as she weighs at age seven. But the lion grows up to be huge—nearly four hundred pounds for adult males, more than two hundred pounds for females. Seventy percent of their diet is meat. Males eat up to fifteen pounds of meat per day, and females up to eleven pounds. She loves learning that females do most of the hunting and that lions rest or sleep almost twenty hours a day.

Later, Hattie discovers that after leaving office, President Theodore Roosevelt and his son, Kermit, led safaris hundreds of miles through Africa for the Smithsonian Museum. In search of the rare white rhino, he and his son trapped thousands of animals to bring back to zoos in America. Seventeen lions were shot in the process; she is sad to read this.

Every week, she gets more books on lions and Africa and eventually other subjects as well. Her thirst for learning seems to be insatiable, and Sarah, Damie, and Jean—her three "mothers"—appear delighted and slightly amused.

Even though they don't have a lot of money, Hattie receives a stuffed lion for her ninth birthday. She names him Adam, actually for Adam and Eve, but Mr. Adams thinks it's after him, and she doesn't correct.

*****

As the oldest son, Henry had inherited forty acres of fertile farmland in Western Kansas when his parents died. He thought that he and Jean might retire there one day, but they realized they were more city people than country folks. His brother, an experienced farmer, wanted to buy the land, so he sold it to him for a decent, brotherly price several years ago. He put the money in the bank and intended for it to be a nest egg for a city retirement someday.

Now he worries because Kansas is experiencing the worst drought in its history, and farms, a huge part of the economy in the late 1920s, are feeling the pinch. His brother assures him he will be okay in spite of the water shortages. Henry worries even more when the stock market crashes on Black Tuesday—October 29, 1929.

CHAPTER 17

Drought, Dust, and Depression

1930–1938

In the early 1930s, Kansas is not experiencing the Depression as badly as most of the rest of the country because it has become a hub for airplane manufacturing and because wheat has a bumper crop. But as the drought worsens, the whole economy begins to suffer. The huge wheat crop of 1931 causes some farmers to be optimistic, but the glut on the market cuts prices drastically and further depresses the economy.

And then it happens. In 1933, the black blizzard starts rolling across the Plains, sweeping the topsoil up into clouds of dust hundreds of feet high. Few provisions have been made for ground cover or other methods to protect the fragile topsoil, and when the winds blow, it goes up like smoke in a wildfire. The economy comes to a standstill, and many have to leave the Dust Bowl that Kansas has become.

*****

Banks all over the country are closing, and the situation is becoming increasingly dire, even for the Adams, who had been enjoying a solid middle-class lifestyle. The bank where Henry works doesn't cut staff at first but soon reduces hours and wages for its employees. Then its doors close altogether, costing Henry both his job and his life savings.

He finds another job at a gas station, but he and Jean are having a hard time making ends meet. The house is paid for, but Henry is not sure how he'll keep the lights on. The dust has destroyed all the vegetables in his garden except a few onions and carrots, and what little food there is in the pantry will probably only sustain them for a few weeks. He's a proud man, but he will stand in line for food if he has to.

The Adams can no longer pay Damie, not even room and board, or have enough to feed the two of them, let alone Damie, Sarah, and Hattie. The diner cuts staff, including Sarah, and she can no longer bring food home from work. She finds odd jobs, but they are scarce and pay next to nothing.

By 1935, the Adams lose everything, and the three guests must leave. They load their few belongings into two pillowcases, three large paper bags, and one suitcase and climb into the back of a bus bound for Tulsa. The tickets cost almost all the money they have saved. Hattie has some dresses and shoes, her books, and her treasured stuffed lion, Adam.

"Momma and Aunt Damie talk about Tulsa and how Greenwood has been rebuilt after the terrible fires and how it's home. Well, it's not home to me," Hattie, now thirteen, complains to herself. "Kansas City is the only home I've known. I like it here. I know everybody is out of work, but I can't imagine it's much better in Tulsa."

Oklahoma is suffering in the early 1930s. One of the worst droughts in history causes both of its two major crops, wheat and corn, to fail. The water shortage is so severe that Oklahoma leaders fear farmers will have to dispose of their cattle because of feed shortages. One farmer runs an ad to give away a hundred hogs rather than watch them starve. Gluts of oil reduce the price, and the economy of the Oil Capital of the World nosedives.

Then the dust starts rolling in from Kansas, and weather from the north means serious trouble. First, hailstorms beat the remaining crops into pebbles and mulch. Close behind come the biggest, blackest clouds anyone has ever seen. High winds do not clear the air, instead filling it with more dust and forcing the dust into every crevice, even making it hard to see something as close as a front porch railing.

Schools close, ponds and lakes dry up and fish die, lung disorders increase exponentially, and traffic and commerce are at a standstill. The Dust Bowl continues to blow strong for three years, causing many Okies to move west.

This is the Tulsa that Damie, Sarah, and Hattie return home to find—no jobs, almost no food, people in worn-out shoes and dresses too small, and no money to buy even used clothes or go to movies or eat out at any of the few establishments not boarded up. No one is in a very positive frame of mind.

Damie knows Sarah cannot take her Black child to her family in white Sand Springs. The two women agree that Damie should take Hattie with her to stay with relatives in Greenwood. Sarah and Hattie are visibly crushed by their sad separation.

Damie is glad Hattie Mae Johnson has a new last name. Everyone knows that Damie is Dick Rowland's aunt, but no one questions the parentage of a stray Colored child in Greenwood during the Depression. Damie is afraid someone will figure out Hattie's true identity but feels relatively safe, for now.

Building on relationships she had prior to leaving almost fifteen years ago, Damie is able to find part-time jobs in Tulsa. Sarah works in her uncle's grocery store in Sand Springs and at any other jobs she can find. Her uncle doesn't pay her much money, but she gets room and board, such as it is. Sarah never tells her family about Hattie.

*****

Sarah and Hattie see each other when they can in Tulsa, usually at Mohawk Park or somewhere they won't be on display, but this doesn't happen often. When they have to part at the end of their time together, both mother and daughter are nearly inconsolable. Hattie loves her aunt Damie and loves to hear stories about when her daddy was young, but she misses her mother every day and cries herself to sleep most every night.

As the years pass, Hattie becomes increasingly curious about her father and wants to know what happened to him. On one of the occasions when they meet, Sarah relents and tells sixteen-year-old Hattie the whole horrible story. Confused, shocked, and angry, Hattie stares at her mother as if she is a stranger. She demands to know why she wasn't told sooner.

"Sweetheart, I'm so sorry, so ashamed. We didn't know what to say or how or when to say it," Sarah admits, sobbing. "We didn't want you to know the sadness and horror of that scene, and like all of Tulsa, we hoped it would just go away."

"You should've told me. It was selfish and cowardly and cruel," Hattie wails. Normally even-tempered, she is angry and shouts through her tears, "It's not fair."

"No, it's not, none of it—not the massacre, not your daddy's murder, us not tellin' you, especially us not tellin' you. I'm sorry, Hattie. It was just all so horrible. We didn't want to lay that burden on you." She pauses, her voice faltering. "And I was so ashamed, am so ashamed, and I didn't want you to blame me, as I have done every day since it happened."

Hattie tries not to blame her mother, but she finds it hard to forgive her momma or her aunt Damie for concealing the truth from her all these years. She now knows that Damie had changed her last name so no one would ever link her to Dick Rowland and the Tulsa riots. She had never questioned this before. Some friends at school in Kansas City had different last names from their mommas or didn't have daddies living with them, so she didn't stick out and hadn't really thought much about it. Now, though she had yearned to know more about the daddy she never met, she doesn't like what she hears.

CHAPTER 18

Best Friends Forever

1935 and Beyond

The Depression is felt keenly by everyone, and no money is available to anyone. With the two biggest industries in Oklahoma—farming and oil—in rapid decline, bank loans dry up as hard as the red dirt. Nearly half of the wealthy homes in South Tulsa are for sale, and there are almost no Colored domestics working there. Yards are overgrown. Even country clubs are nearly abandoned.

Sand Springs suffers more than most. Oil is its only industry, and without that, people are starving. A few grocery stores are all that's left, and any semblance of sanitation has gone to hell. As white Tulsa suffers, employment and incomes in Greenwood also plummet.

By the time Hattie, Sarah, and Damie arrive, Greenwood has largely been rebuilt. However, thanks to the Depression, the former Black Wall Street is mostly an economic wasteland. Few stores and hardly any movies or dining establishments are open because no one has money to buy anything.

Despite the hard times, Sarah and Damie set aside any money they can—often skipping meals—to save for Hattie to go to college. But times are rougher than anyone has ever endured, and money is scarce. Everybody minds their own business and learns the value of a nickel.

Hattie works two days at a restored Black church watching little ones who have no adults at home—the few lucky ones who have jobs. She also works two afternoons at the library, one of the first buildings to catch fire in 1921 and one of the first to reopen the following year.

Fire is the enemy of books, and the library lost almost all of its books and periodicals. The shelves are still only half full, and the supply of reading materials is pretty meager, but this is the job Hattie loves, even with not so many books. She devours the few that the library has and helps repair and catalog books they receive from the white library and some white churches. It's not much, but it's something to work with.

She works at the church and the library almost four years before she can finally go to Booker T. Washington High School. She is almost seventeen and it is 1939. There, she excels and meets her first, new, and only best friend, Lucy Ann Barnes.

*****

Like Hattie, Lucy is the product of an interracial couple, a shared reality that binds the two teenagers almost immediately.

Lucy's Black mother, Violet, worked for a Coach Palmer at Oklahoma Agricultural and Mechanical College (later Oklahoma State University) where she met Lucy's white father, Tom. Her mother had told Lucy he was that blue-eyed, blond kind of handsome, and he was fun and kind. A World War I veteran, he was a wrestler for the college and hung out at the coach's house, meaning he was often around Violet. They dated secretly and fell in love.

Violet had been saving her money because she intended to take classes at Oklahoma Colored Agricultural and Normal University (later Langston University) twenty-six miles from Oklahoma A&M and next door to her hometown, Pleasant Valley. It was the only Black college in Oklahoma, and Blacks were prohibited by law from attending any white college in the state for decades.

When Violet became pregnant, her dreams of higher education disappeared. She was disappointed but always saw Lucy as a gift from God. Tom could not tell his family what had happened, especially since Violet was not white, but she made him promise to help with their child's education. She moved to Oklahoma City as soon as she started to show, to a Black neighborhood called Deep Deuce, north of Bricktown, north of Second Street.

There was employment in Oklahoma City in the 1920s thanks largely to the oil boom. Coach Palmer had written Violet a good reference letter, partly as a favor to his star wrestler, and she got work with a kind white family who treated her well and didn't judge—or at least didn't openly criticize—her situation. Tom helped as best he could.

*****

As Lucy grows up, the Depression hits Oklahoma City especially hard because the opening of the East Texas Oil Field creates a disastrous glut on the market. The price of a barrel is cut almost by half, and employment rolls are reduced by more than that. Violet loses her job. There is no public assistance. Will Rogers gives benefit performances, and the Red Cross, the Salvation Army, and church groups do what they can.

Lucy's father sends a little bit of money every two weeks to Violet. Once he starts working in the family business, Violet can write him there about what is going on and how well Lucy is doing in elementary school. She tells him he can send them money in care of the Calvary Baptist Church, which they attend nearly every Sunday in good times and bad.

As the Depression worsens, Violet and Lucy are forced to move out of Deep Deuce and into a Hooverville, derogatorily named after President Herbert Hoover, on the south bank of the North Canadian River. The river frequently overflows its banks, increasing disease and magnifying the overall odious condition of the place. Violet never tells Tom how squalid their situation is, and she never complains or says anything bad about him to Lucy. In fact, she hardly says anything about him at all. Lucy barely knows his name—Tom Jackson.

When Lucy gets a little older, she works any job she can find, but there aren't many, and she can't even go to school for a while. Eventually, as the Depression wanes a bit and the economy slowly picks up, Violet moves with Lucy to Greenwood, where tales of Black Wall Street are legendary. Since the excellent Fredrick Douglas High School had been moved to east, Oklahoma City, Violet decides Booker T. Washington will be a good school for Lucy.

She begins high school in the fall of 1939 and meets Hattie Johnson almost immediately. After only a few weeks, Hattie tells Lucy about the Greenwood Riot and the roles her mother and father played in sparking the horrific events. On that day, they become Best Friends Forever.

*****

Hattie and Lucy both love school. They can't afford to join any extracurricular activities, but most of the other kids can't either. The books are old and tattered and have many pages missing. The teachers, though very strict, are determined, and so are Hattie and Lucy. Hattie graduates at the top of the class of 1941. Lucy is second, and all three proud mommas—Sarah, Damie, and Violet—are there to see their babies take top honors.

The economy improves a bit more after Hattie completes high school—what with the war and all—but it still takes another year of working, borrowing, and saving. Finally, using money that she, Sarah, and Damie have saved, she's off to her first year in college with a slightly tattered Adam in tow.

Immediately after high school, Lucy goes to Howard University in Washington DC with help from RWD (rich white daddy), whom she never meets. He has gone into his father's construction business in Louisiana, Violet tells her, and is doing well enough to help his daughter. Howard is by far the best Black college in the country, and her mother and father agree that's where she must go. Tom sets up a scholarship fund at Howard, and Lucy is the only recipient. Later, she exchanges infrequent letters with RWD, especially after her mother dies.

By the early 1940s, there are some good Black colleges in Oklahoma. However, Hattie opts for Paul Quinn College, a private school in Waco, Texas, affiliated with the African Methodist

Episcopal Church. Because Quinn is a work-study college, Hattie literally works her way through school, which she does as a teaching assistant. The money that she, her mother, and her aunt saved helps pay for books, room and board, and other expenses not covered by her work-study. There's even a little leftover for an occasional movie and her minimal fees and dues for membership in Alpha Kappa Alpha plus a few dollars to put away for teacher's college after graduation.

Lucy visits her twice at Paul Quinn, and they have a time. They splurge on ice cream, dance with Adam, and laugh until they nearly wet their pants. Lucy had also joined Alpha Kappa Alpha at Howard, and they laugh hysterically over the secret handshake and password.

Hattie's aunt Damie sends her money for a bus home when Lucy's mother dies in an automobile accident. Damie helps with the arrangements while Lucy and Hattie make their separate, sad trips back to Tulsa for the funeral. It's the only time Hattie makes the trip back to Tulsa during her years at Paul Quinn—to support her best friend in her despondency.

Neither Damie nor Sarah can come to Waco to see her graduate with honors from Paul Quinn after only two years. Lucy can't be there either, as she is already in law school at Howard. But Hattie doesn't really mind. She has found her calling as a teacher, though only an assistant, and goes immediately to Langston University for her teacher's certificate.

At Langston, Hattie meets the strikingly handsome Andrew Rogers, a slightly older World War II veteran, who was discharged in 1944 after suffering a minor injury. He promptly steals Hattie's twenty-two-year-old heart. Andrew grew up just outside of Tulsa and plans to begin a career there as an auto mechanic. A bit of a poet and philosopher, he puts off his mechanic's career to attend a year or two of college. Also, he wants his children to be educated but not be too much smarter than he is. Both Hattie and Andrew think they are too old to partake of Greek life at Langston, although they do attend a couple of Alpha Kappa Alpha alumni dinners and dances.

Hattie graduates from Langston in 1945 at the top of her class, as usual, even though she had to work two jobs. Damie and Sarah make the trip to Langston for the graduation ceremony with the added bonus of meeting Hattie's Andrew for the first time. Lucy is in the thick of finals and cannot be there but sends a note saying she'll take Hattie to dinner when they both get home.

She and Andrew marry as soon as school is out and as soon as Lucy can get there. The wedding is a small affair in the backyard of the home Damie now rents in Greenwood. Andrew refuses to wear his uniform and opts for a lightweight, single-breasted charcoal-gray suit with soft-blue shirt and solid-blue tie.

The women do not simplify. Both mothers of the bride wear fashionable suits, Damie in orange and Sarah in light mauve blue with double-breasted buttons on the bodice and down the skirt. Lucy, home from law school, is maid of honor and wears a typically sensible beige linen suit with matching heels.

Hattie, of course, steals the show in a simple, sleeveless white sheath with a chiffon scarf and hip bow of mauve blue to match Sarah's suit. She has purchased a matching box jacket she plans to wear when she teaches in the spring knowing sleeveless will not be proper teacher attire. Teardrop earrings and a necklace borrowed from Damie complete the ensemble. Andrew cannot take his eyes off her.

Sarah tearfully gives away the bride. After a brief ceremony, all enjoy homemade cake, fried chicken, stewed okra with tomatoes and onions, and potato salad. Dick's friend Jimmy Henderson is there too, and he introduces Andrew to the men at the Williams Garage, which he now partly owns.

*****

Hattie is hired at Washington High School the minute she finishes her teacher's certificate in 1945. She and Andrew eventually have two sons, Ernest and Harvey, both of whom attend four-year colleges and bless them with beautiful grandchildren.

Lucy meets Harold Wilson at Howard law school, and they marry shortly after graduating in 1948. The couple sets up a law practice in Tulsa, returning to the Greenwood neighborhood where

Lucy spent her teenage years. They eventually have two children—Nola and Elroy—and two wonderful grandchildren.

From the 1950s on, the two best friends are together again, forever.

CHAPTER 19

Don't Expect Nuthin'

2001–2005

After the report from the Commission to Study the Tulsa Race Riot of 1921 fails to generate significant action by Oklahoma and Tulsa officials in 2001, the dream team ramps up its work. In 2003, after months of intense preparation and with help from Lucy and Hattie, the team sues, arguing that survivors and descendants are entitled to "restitution and reparations for injuries due to the actions and inactions of Tulsa and Oklahoma officials" in 1921.

Later that year, the District Court for the Northern District of Oklahoma finds Tulsa and Oklahoma officials responsible for the damage and injuries suffered by the citizens of Greenwood because they "routinely underinvestigated, underresponded, mishandled, and failed to protect" the victims "from a series of criminal acts or to prosecute those responsible for such acts."

Nonetheless, the court refuses to grant any compensation for victims or reparations of any kind due to the statute of limitations. Later, the Tenth District Court of Appeals upholds the statute of limitations and refuses to hear the case.

"There are no words, Miss Hattie," the crestfallen Wilbur McNeely tells Lucy and Hattie in his Tulsa office. "This is the new millennium, yet we might as well be living under the old Jim Crow. When we took the old ladies to the appeals court in Denver, I really thought we had a shot. Representative Ross thought we had a shot.

Johnnie Cochrane and Charles Ogletree thought we had a shot. Charlie Crabtree worked relentlessly to prepare an ironclad case, and I know you two were right by his side the entire way." Lucy nods, thinking about her tireless research into relevant cases.

"Those ladies were ready to tell their stories," Wilbur continues angrily, "how respectable white thugs broke into their homes and their wives came behind them with pillowcases, shopping bags, and shipping crates to steal their valuables before burning their homes to the ground. Shopping bags and shipping crates!" He repeats for emphasis.

"It's a travesty, Wilbur," Lucy agrees. "These women are eyewitnesses."

"But the court refused to hear the case due to the statute of limitations—"

"Just an excuse," Lucy interrupts. "And there should be no statute of limitations on mass murder."

"Maybe the Supreme Court will make this right, Wilbur," Hattie says hopefully. "The Supremes have straightened out some things in the past."

"But some of these ladies may not last that long."

"You're a good man, Wilbur. You keep on tryin'. That's why Don trusts you so much."

*****

Within two years, *Greenwood v. the State of Oklahoma* is on the docket of the Supreme Court of the United States. The intervening time had demanded intense research by all involved, reading and rereading cases and precedents, and preparing briefs late into nearly every night. Most Tulsans, white and Black, are virtually unaware of the lawsuit, relegating this—as has been done since 1921—to a chapter of Oklahoma history best forgotten.

On May 16, 2005, a reporter standing on the steps of the highest court in the land speaks directly into the camera: "Four disappointed ninety-year-olds were told by this court today that after nearly eighty-five years, they will not be heard. The Supreme Court today upheld the Tenth District Court and refused to hear *Greenwood v. the State of Oklahoma* on grounds that the statute of limitations had run out long ago. How do you feel about this, Representative Ross?"

"You know and I know there is no damn statute of limitations on a moral obligation," Don replies in an authoritative, enraged voice. "The facts of the case are documented and irrefutable: Tulsa police and the local National Guard recruited and armed white men and told them to round up all the men of Greenwood, which they did, leaving the community virtually defenseless. Then these officials and their new recruits proceeded to murder, rob, and incinerate nearly forty square blocks of a thriving African American community known as Black Wall Street.

"After that, the town fathers established laws making it legally impossible for Black homeowners and businesses to rebuild. They did so anyway against all odds. No Black insurance claim has ever been honored, although many white claims were paid. This is the twenty-first century. We expected more from the highest damn court in our land. This is our country too. When are you people going to stop treating us like we don't belong here?"

Watching the coverage with Lucy, Hattie repeats the bitter words of her aunt's disabled friend, Hiram Porter: "Well, like Uncle Hiram used to say, don't expect nuthin' and you won't be disappointed."

CHAPTER 20

Raising the Dead

2005

After years of denials and delays, the city of Tulsa finally unearths a mass grave in Oaklawn Cemetery on Eleventh and Peoria where the remains of no fewer than two hundred African Americans were dumped in 1921. Dick Rowland's remains are among those identified thanks to DNA testing and the diamond in his front tooth.

Due to the numerous court cases and hearings on reparations for those affected by the riots, Tulsa officials knew Hattie Johnson Rogers was Dick's daughter. She recently provided a sample of her DNA for matching purposes, just in case.

When she hears the news, Hattie is overcome with emotion. As usual, Lucy provides comfort and support. The two women discuss what should be done, given that the remains are too decomposed to be moved. Finally, Hattie decides to go to Sand Springs to bring her momma home to rest next to Dick.

*****

Woodland Memorial Park Cemetery had been in Sand Springs for nearly a hundred years. When Hattie's mother died, she had to make all the decisions, as there were no living relatives to take care of the funeral arrangements or perhaps be disgraced by the presence of Sarah's Black love child. The Page family had a plot at Woodland,

144

and Hattie sadly remembers burying her mother there on a stormy autumn day in 1984. Andrew, Ernest and Harvey, Lucy and Harold, and Nola and Elroy were the only people with her at that somber scene. She would not have been able to make it without them.

"Momma was almost eighty years old. It seems longer than twenty-one years ago that we buried her here," Hattie tells Lucy as they plan their next steps. "Aunt Damie preceded momma by eight years, but the two of them remained my guardian angels until the end."

Damie had moved in with Andrew and Hattie when Ernest was born. Andrew worked long hours in Williams Garage during those years and became part owner just before Jimmy retired. All had agreed to keep the Williams name out of respect for the Greenwood forefather.

Once Damie moved in, Hattie was able to go back to teaching, at least until Harvey was born. Besides, Hattie liked the company, and Damie knew a thing or two about raising rambunctious little boys. She helped keep them in line as they went through their rebellious teens. They were actually pretty good boys, and they had to study hard because their momma was the teacher, Hattie chuckled to herself.

Aloud, she continues reminiscing with Lucy. "It was easier to see Momma in those later years. Bus service had picked up, and the cable line was back in business. Andrew would always drive her back to Sand Springs at the end of the day. It still hurt to separate, but the boys kept me pretty busy, and they loved the time they spent with their Gramma."

Hattie and Sarah saw each other most Saturdays—always in Tulsa, often picnicking at Mohawk Park, usually with Hattie's kids and sometimes with Lucy and one or both of her children. When Sarah took everyone to the zoo, Damie would tell stories about Hattie's early fascination with the animals.

"Remember how Aunt Damie said she thought I might become a vet the way I carried on about the animals?" Hattie reminds Lucy. "She would ask over and over, 'Whatever happened to your lion, Adam?' And I told her every time that he finally lost his eyes and one of his legs and that I buried him in the backyard. Seeing Momma was always bittersweet, sometimes sad, sometimes a little strained, but I never doubted her love for me."

"She told me many times how very proud she was of you," Lucy replies, lending comfort and support as always.

The two friends had often wondered why Sarah stayed in Sand Springs all those years. "No place else to go, I guess," Lucy once suggested, though she undoubtedly knew Hattie and Andrew would have made room for Sarah, even with Damie living there.

Sarah had remained an attractive woman, and Hattie used to wonder why she never dated or got married. But as time passed, Hattie understood. Sarah never got over the deep guilt or the oppressive shame. She had no guilt or shame about loving Dick, but the overwhelming remorse and regret about the riot, its aftermath, and Dick's murder often depressed her to exhaustion.

Sarah had told Hattie she was glad she didn't know any details of Dick's death. She said she barely looked at his attackers while she fled because she knew she would have been killed—or worse—if she had returned or tried to get help. But Hattie knew self-reproach filled every sinew of her mother's soul. Greenwood was destroyed, Dick was gone. He never got to meet his daughter. And Sarah never got over any of it.

*****

Today, Hattie and sons Ernest and Harvey, Lucy and son Elroy (Nola is on a mission in Xi'an, China), and all four adult grandchildren gather, along with Rep. Don Ross, legislative aide Wilbur McNeely, and Atty. Charlie Crabtree, to witness the exhumation of Sarah's cherrywood casket from its deep resting place.

The trip from Woodland to Oaklawn Cemetery seems interminable, but the group finally arrives and proceeds to the recently unearthed mass grave. Hattie thinks she couldn't cry anymore, but the years of separation from her mother, never knowing her father, and the passing of her momma and her aunt Damie all well up in her like a roaring waterfall, and the tears gush like the oil that founded her beloved and cursed city.

Swallowing her sobs and leaning on Lucy, as she has always done in grief and in joy, Hattie thanks Don, Wilbur, and Atty. Crabtree for making it possible to identify her father and to bring her mother's casket to Oaklawn to be with him.

Don looks down into the open gravesite as he begins his remarks. "We cannot redress the grievances done to the young lovers Dick and Sarah, and we cannot undo the irreparable damage caused by their ill-fated love. But today, by finally reuniting them in death, we can begin to mend our own hearts that have been ripped asunder.

"We know Sarah had a full life, though many times it was difficult. She was able to endure the worst and cared for those she loved through it all. She worked and saved and put money away so that her daughter would have a better life. She was beloved by her daughter, grandchildren, all of us gathered here today, and the many others whose lives she touched."

Now both Hattie and Lucy are tearful. Lucy had gotten to know Sarah in later years and spent time with her when she was dying in Sand Springs. Once Don is finished, Charlie Crabtree takes his turn. "This mass grave is an indelible symbol of the dehumanization of one race by another, which unfortunately continues today. These two lovers didn't see the color, but they felt its awesome weight, and they gave the world this lovely woman, Hattie, who has been such a boon to this community.

"We shall never forget what happened here, and we will continue to fight for the rights of our people through all adversity and discrimination with the good guidance of leaders like Representative Don Ross and the constant support of people like Hattie and Lucy and their families. They are a beautiful reminder to us all that no matter what life throws at you, you are not alone."

Sarah's casket is placed beside Dick's remains, which have been carefully wrapped in a clean white cloth. Dirt is thrown over the two lovers, and a place-saving grave marker is put at the top of the yet-to-be-filled pit. At the end of the service, Hattie thanks all her family for their undying support. "I could not have done this without your love and loyalty."

*****

As is the tradition after a graveside service, Hattie, Lucy, and the rest of the group go to their home for a light meal, sweet tea, dessert, and conversation. The subject of the hour—second only to how great Sarah was—is the recent refusal of the Supreme Court to hear their case.

"It never ends," Lucy laments. "Everyone says Tulsa and Oklahoma state officials were guilty, negligent, and downright criminal, but no one will stand up for the people who have no voice, the community who lost their birthright and their hard-won successes, all dashed by greedy realtors and drunk white trash. Yet no one is held accountable."

"But you can be proud of all you and Harold have done for the children of Greenwood, Lucy," Hattie reassuringly tells her and the others gathered in their home. "Fifty Washington High School graduates are on full four-year college scholarships thanks to the fund you established."

"Well, you know we could not have gotten that done without your help and persistent dogging of donors," Lucy responds, always quick to give Hattie the credit she richly deserves.

It is not what the two best friends had hoped for—all the scholarship money had come from private donations, including their own. Still, Lucy, Hattie, and the others who worked so tirelessly on reparations had given a hand up to Black kids who needed it, kids who should be proud of their color, their heritage, and their accomplishments.

Before the guests leave, all in attendance join Hattie and Lucy in a final pledge: "Anything resembling the Tulsa Race Massacre of 1921 must happen *Never Again!*"

EPILOGUE

2020

Most Americans had never heard of the Tulsa Race Massacre of 1921 until a COVID-19 super-spreader rally was scheduled in Tulsa on Juneteenth, the day that celebrates when Texas slaves were told they were free—June 19, 1865, two and a half years after the Emancipation Proclamation. Due to public outrage, the tone-deaf campaign event for then President Donald J. Trump was rescheduled for another date.

Even Tulsans have found it too easy to forget that up to three hundred Blacks were murdered and forty blocks of one of the most affluent African American communities in the country incinerated in less than twenty-four hours by a white mob with the near total complicity of local National Guard, police, and civic officials. This is—at least partially—because the Tulsa Race Massacre, also known as the Race Riot of 1921, and all the impediments to rebuilding the decimated district were carefully and deliberately buried, erased and concealed for decades.

The inflammatory article announcing a lynching for the night of May 31, 1921, was removed from the archives of the *Tulsa Tribune*. The Tulsa Historical Society kept no photographs or accounts of the Massacre for years. City documents, including police reports, went missing. Meanwhile, though more than two thousand Black families lived in tents in the winter of 1921 and 1922, the city of Tulsa zoned much of Greenwood for a new rail depot.

*****

The day after the Massacre, the Tulsa Reparations Committee began work on "retrieving the proud name of Tulsa," according to news reports. An all-white public welfare board promised financial support and asked the Red Cross to fund the cost of relief personnel. In less than two weeks, Mayor T. D. Evans dissolved the board. A new board subsequently refused all offers of assistance by agencies from across the country and around the world. Instead, they began local fundraising efforts, and a few wealthy Tulsans funded the Red Cross efforts.

This high commission of seven white civic leaders promised that "every effort will be made" to "make good" the Massacre victims' "losses." Newspapers reported that representatives from the Commission condemned city and county law enforcement officials for failure to perform in a professional manner during the violence. A committee was appointed to "care for the more than three thousand helpless Negroes and to expedite rebuilding the burned Negro quarter."

In truth, efforts to keep these promises were never begun. Maurice Willows, head of the Red Cross rescue effort in Tulsa in 1921 and 1922, wrote that the Commission was working to take Negro properties and establish a new Negro district farther away from white Tulsa with a commercial/industrial district separating the two communities. The Red Cross and, especially, Willows were heralded as angels of mercy in the Greenwood community.

When out-of-town journalists arrived in Tulsa, many assumed that whites—even though they had gathered in an apparent lynch mob—were not totally to blame for the initial outbreak at the Tulsa County Courthouse or for the shocking destruction that followed on May 31 and June 1. However, it soon became clear to them that the fighting had pushed the Coloreds back to Greenwood and that the threat of a Negro uprising, if there ever was one, had ended, well before the worst of the Massacre began.

Compared to millions of dollars in Greenwood, only about forty thousand dollars in damage was done to the white business district, virtually all of it by whites. Journalists soon realized that an estimated ten to fifteen thousand armed white mobsters had launched a white invasion—by land and by air—on June 1. In the opinion of the *New York Times*, for example, "The ruthless demolition of virtually the entire Negro quarter north of the tracks is condemned as indefensible violence."

Despite the national condemnation, Tulsa mayor Evans appeared to back the wanton destruction of Greenwood: "It was good generalship to let the destruction come to that section where the trouble was hatched up...and where it had its inception."

Some Tulsa officials had a different point of view. Former Mayor Loyal Martin, for example, took the position that "Tulsa can only redeem itself from the country-wide shame and humiliation...by complete restitution and rehabilitation of the destroyed Black belt."

Expressing support for reparations, Martin continued. "We have neglected our duties, and our city government has fallen down. The city and county are legally responsible for every dollar of the damage that has been done. Other cities have had to pay [for] race riots, and we shall have to...because we have neglected our duty as citizens."

Within two months, the KKK had a burning cross-initiation of over a thousand new members in Tulsa, bringing the Oklahoma total to nearly one hundred thousand, more than the entire empire had been nationally just a few years before. Within eighteen months, Tulsa became home to the holding company for the Knights of the Ku Klux Klan, the Benevolent Association of Tulsa. In 1922, the brotherhood's three-story, steel reinforced, whitewashed stucco Klavern / BENO Hall towered ominously over the tents of hundreds of Black Tulsans still homeless from the destruction of Greenwood.

BENO supposedly stood for the Benevolent Organization. However, in local parlance and in reality, it meant *Be No* Nigger, *Be No* Catholic, *Be No* Jew, *Be No* Immigrant. For much of the next four decades, the brotherhood terrorized and victimized these four groups at work, at worship, and at home. Tulsa boasted a youth group of the KKK and its first women's auxiliary. In 1924, KKK candidates won all of Tulsa's city offices.

*****

For the most part, the true story of what happened in the Tulsa Race Massacre of 1921 remained untold for years. In fact, the story was emphatically erased from most of the collective memory of Tulsa, the state of Oklahoma, and the wider nation at large.

Then as the fiftieth anniversary of the Massacre approached, Larry Silvey, editor of the Chamber of Commerce's *Tulsa Magazine*, commissioned local historian Ed Wheeler to write the Race Riot story. A former US Army brigadier general and captain in the Oklahoma National Guard, Wheeler was meticulous in his research. He dutifully granted anonymity to all sources who requested it, and almost all did. As news spread of Wheeler's project, threats were made against him and his family. At six foot four, two hundred and thirty-five pounds, Wheeler was not afraid, but he moved his wife and son to a safer location.

After months of interviews and poring over thousands of pages and photographs documenting the event, Wheeler turned in his story to Silvey. According to many accounts (including James Hirsch's *Riot and Remembrance*), Clyde Cole, head of the Tulsa Chamber of Commerce, told Silvey he could not publish the article. When Wheeler went to Cole's office and complained, Cole said the story would start a race riot.

Both the *Tulsa World* and *Tulsa Tribune* refused the story on the same grounds. However, a new Black magazine called *Impact* had recently appeared in Tulsa, and its editor was civil rights advocate Don Ross. *Impact* published the story in June of 1971. Few white Tulsans ever saw the article, but the true story had finally surfaced, and more articles, documentaries, and books gradually appeared.

*****

Maxine Horner, a Booker T. Washington High School graduate who served in the Oklahoma Senate from 1986 to 2004 and died in February 2021, wrote eloquently about the catastrophe in her native Tulsa:

> After the epitaph for the Black boulevard was written in flames, the aftermath led more toward conspiracy to further dehumanize the suffering population than to demonstrate justice... Hopefully, generations of today and tomorrow are the persuasive custodians of a moral recovery, driven to disperse a forgiving, fair, kind, humane, deserved, and final closure—with decent justice. To do nothing leaves us to condone the error, murder, mob rule, lawlessness, racism, and even more hideously intolerant teachings. The piety of piled-on indifference vanquishes our morality as the poetry of hypocrites, the treachery of which is lost on the commandments of a good God.

In 2001, the report from the Oklahoma Commission to Study the Tulsa Race Riot of 1921 recommended that "after multiple acts of horror," the following reparations should be made:

- Direct payments to survivors and descendants
- A scholarship fund for students affected by the riot
- A memorial for victims and the burial of remains of the victims
- A Development Enterprise Zone in historic Greenwood

Regarding the Commission's recommendations on "direct payments to survivors and descendants" and on "a scholarship fund for students affected by the riot:"

To date, no reparations from public money have been paid to any survivors or descendants of the 1921 Tulsa Race Massacre. Nor have public funds financed scholarships for students affected by the riot."

In 1994, Florida passed a law that allows descendants of the 1923 Rosewood Massacre to go to any college in the state tuition free. So far, this is the only instance of a legislative body in the United States giving reparations to African Americans. However, the US paid reparations for slavery to white slave owners in compensation for the loss of their slave property after the Civil War. By contrast, within one month of the bombing of the Alfred P. Murrah Federal Building on April 19, 1995, a group of eighty agencies convened and started meeting weekly to determine and help fill unmet victim needs stemming from the bombing. This group continued to meet five years later to review requests from victims, survivors, family members, and disaster workers and allocate a significant, albeit decreasing, supply of funds.

Other contrasts include the outpouring of help, reconstruction, and compensation after the horrific 9-11 attacks in 2001 and the $800 million settlement quickly reached for victims of the 2018 mass shooting in Las Vegas where fifty-eight people died—all deserved and all achieved swiftly without substantial controversy. In each of these instances, victims were predominantly white.

The John Hope Franklin Tulsa-Greenwood Race Riot Claims Accountability Act, initially introduced in the US House of Representatives in 2013, has been reintroduced in both houses of Congress. The act would create a new opportunity for a federal cause of action to provide reparations to those deprived of their civil rights during and after the Massacre and to prosecute the people responsible.

Regarding the Commission's recommendation on "a memorial for victims and for the burial of remains of the victims":
Until recently, memorials to the Massacre victims were funded almost exclusively by private donations. But in 2019, Tulsa voters approved $5.34 million, and the state committed $1.5 million for the $30 million Greenwood Rising History Center building. It is scheduled to be completed by Memorial Day 2021, the centennial of the Tulsa Race Massacre. Originally planned for construction next

to the Greenwood Cultural Center, the History Center site was relocated to the historic southeast corner of Greenwood and Archer.

Thanks primarily to private donations from Black and white Tulsans, a few memorials had already been built, by the year 2020. The Greenwood Cultural Center was dedicated in 1995. Its stated mission is "promoting, preserving, and celebrating African American culture and heritage," focusing in particular on the 1921 Tulsa race Massacre, Black Wall Street, and the remembrances of survivors.

"This horrific event affected the lives and culture of many people in North Tulsa," stated Frances Jordan-Rakestraw, executive director of the Greenwood Cultural Center. "We need to know this history so that such an event will never happen again."

John Hope Franklin Reconciliation Park was built in 2009. A twenty-five-foot tower at the center of the park depicts some of the struggles of African Americans in Oklahoma history—the migration of slaves on the Trail of Tears, the slave labor experience in Oklahoma Territories, the First Kansas Colored Volunteer Infantry that won the Battle of Honey Springs, the immigration of free Blacks into Oklahoma after statehood, and the all-Black towns of Oklahoma, including Greenwood. Renamed in 2010, the park honors Dr. John Hope Franklin, a renowned historian and author who graduated from Booker T. Washington High School, and also his grandfather B. C. Franklin, a prominent Black attorney who defended survivors of the 1921 Massacre.

On August 16, 2019, a memorial to Ellis Walker Woods, first principal of Booker T. Washington High School, was unveiled on the Oklahoma State University-Tulsa campus near the site of the original high school. The memorial includes sixty-two granite pillars bearing the images of important figures in the school's history.

In contrast to the long-awaited Greenwood memorials, President Bill Clinton signed the Oklahoma City Memorial Act within two years. The Oklahoma City Bombing Memorial was formally dedicated on April 19, 2000, exactly five years after the devastating bombing. The outdoor memorial, on three acres where the Alfred P. Murrah Building once stood, consists of a reflecting pool and a field of 168 chairs commemorating the victims, including nineteen smaller chairs for the children at Kids Day Care Center. The chairs are made of glass and bronze, and each victim's name is etched on one chair. State and federal governments provided $10 million, and private donations totaled $17 million.

In Tulsa, the search for the buried remains of race riot victims continues. On October 23, 2020, remains were found in what appeared to be a mass grave at Oaklawn Cemetery. Experts said it was too early to connect those remains with victims of the 1921 Massacre. However, many close to the investigation are optimistic.

In May of 2021, the privately funded Tulsa Community Remembrance Coalition plans to erect the first comprehensive, public memorial honoring victims of the 1921 Tulsa Massacre on the grounds of the rebuilt Vernon African Methodist Episcopal Church. Every Wednesday, AME pastor Reverend Robert Turner leads a procession to City Hall demanding "reparations now!"

Regarding the Commission's recommendation on Development Enterprise Zone *in historic Greenwood*:

In 2019, the Greenwood-Unity Heritage Neighborhood Sector Urban Renewal Plan was the reason for a meeting attended by hundreds of Greenwood residents adamantly opposed to the city's plan. The plan would have further displaced Greenwood residents by raising rents to unaffordable levels for current businesses and residences. The Tulsa Development Authority suspended its plans.

*****

Despite unbelievable obstacles, Greenwood had the grit to fight back and rise up—even though out-numbered, out-gunned and out-planned—and the grit to rebuild, beating a system intent on beating them down.

By the end of 1921, Greenwood residents had rebuilt more than eight hundred structures in the neighborhood. By June of 1922, after many residents spent a bitter winter in tents, virtually all the area's homes had been replaced. Black builders secured supplies from nearby states, and within a year, most of the buildings on Greenwood

Avenue were rebuilt in spite of the best efforts of white officials, businessmen, banks, and insurance companies.

In 1925, Greenwood hosted the National (Black) Business League Annual Meeting. The following year, W. E. B. DuBois, noted Harvard-educated sociologist, civil rights icon, writer, orator, and a founder of the NAACP, declared, "Black Tulsa is a happy city. It has new clothes. It is young and gay and strong. Five little years ago, fire, blood and robbery leveled it to the ground. Scars are there, but the city is impudent and noisy. It believes in itself. Thank God for the grit of Black Tulsa."

By the 1930s, the economy of Greenwood was reasonably solid again despite rocky years during the Depression and Dust Bowl. Ironically, Greenwood and other Black communities suffered setbacks due to Pres. Franklin Roosevelt's New Deal, which inadvertently provided a road map for banks and loan companies to institute redlining. Nevertheless, Black schools and churches soon began catering to Greenwood, once again demonstrating against all odds the resilience and resourcefulness of the African American people.

Black Wall Street was thriving in Greenwood by the 1940s, again thanks to severe segregation creating the need for local services for district residents. The Greenwood Chamber of Commerce listed hundreds of Black-owned businesses and called Greenwood "unquestionably the greatest assembly of Negro shops and stores to be found anywhere in America." The Mt. Zion Baptist Church, rebuilt with love and the privately funded repayment of the loan taken out to build it originally, was dedicated on October 21, 1952, thirty-one years after hatred destroyed it.

Greenwood had risen from the ashes of destruction caused by hate and fear. It rose above the Depression, the dust storms, and brutal unemployment of that era, but it could not persevere against desegregation and urban renewal. In the 1960s, the Greenwood area was designated as the location for a major freeway, separating the community from itself just as there were more opportunities for Blacks to move out of Greenwood and into better school districts and areas with nicer homes, amenities, and shopping. A new generation, not beholden to the concept, began leaving Greenwood, perhaps for dead. Interstate 244 was the final nail in the coffin. This confluence of progress had all but extinguished the bright light that once was Black Wall Street.

*****

Despite setbacks, Blacks continued to make slow but steady progress in Tulsa and elsewhere throughout Oklahoma. The Calvary Baptist Church in the Deep Deuce district of Oklahoma City was the site of many activities of the Civil Rights Movement in the1950s, including the student sit-in at the Katz Drug Store lunch counter in 1958. The forty-third annual convention of the NAACP was held at the Calvary Baptist Church around that time.

In the Rotunda of the Oklahoma State Capitol hang portraits of several notable Oklahoma Black men, including Dr. John Hope Franklin, his grandfather B. C. Franklin, and Benjamin Harrison Hill, the first African American elected to the Oklahoma Legislature in 1968.

On October 25, 1996, J. B. Stradford, prominent Greenwood businessman and one of more than sixty-five Black men indicted for inciting the Massacre, was cleared of wrongdoing, and all charges were dropped. Stradford's descendants came from all over the country to witness the ceremony. Gov. Keating noted at the ceremony that the departure of the Stradford family was a tragic loss to Oklahoma.

This long-overdue acquittal was set in motion when Stradford's great grandson Cornelius E. Toole, circuit court judge in Cook County, Illinois, contacted Rep. Don Ross after seeing Bryant Gumbel's report on the Tulsa Race Massacre on the *Today Show*. Toole explained to Rep. Ross that Stradford had actually tried to quell the riots. Ross asked Tulsa County District Attorney Bill LaFortune to reexamine the case. He did and found Stradford to be not guilty. This was seventy-five years after the Massacre and sixty years after the exiled Stradford, who lost his fortune in 1921, had died in Chicago.

Three Tulsa brothers (Charlie, Ronnie, and Robert Wilson) formed the GAP band, which was popular in the 1970s and 1980s. The name came from Greenwood, Archer, and Pine. A thriving

Tulsa Arts District now stands back-to-back with Greenwood. The district previously had been named after Tate Brady, a wealthy civic leader and KKK member involved in the Massacre, but the name was changed in 2017. Trendy new soul food eateries and music festivals have replaced the diners and maids' day off promenades of old.

Veneice Sims, who had missed her prom in 1921, was elected Prom Queen for Booker T. Washington High School in 2000. In February of 2020, Oklahoma state superintendent Joy Hofmeister said the state's public schools would introduce the Tulsa Race Massacre into their Oklahoma history curriculum. That same month, Tulsa appointed its first Black police chief, Wendell Franklin, a twenty-three-year veteran of the Tulsa Police Department.

*****

It is easy, or at least commonplace, to try to reconcile the criminal actions of those in the past with moral values of today by claiming it was a different time, the Jim Crow Era or whatever. But in reality, moral values do not change. Fashion changes, attitudes change, politics change, and climate certainly changes. But morals are the internal compass that guide the lives of moral human beings. It is not trendy or popular. It is right and just.

Unfortunately, the parallels between the Tulsa Race Massacre of 1921 and the insurrection at the US Capitol on January 6, 2021, are striking. White supremacy was at the core of both deadly events. Frightened and angry white men were the primary perpetrators, seemingly fearful that Blacks, Liberal Democrats, or anyone who did not support Donald J. Trump's bid to overturn the election would take over their country. Sadly, the reaction of authorities in both instances was to deal leniently or not at all with white rioters and to be especially harsh with Black Americans.

In May of 2020, the Human Rights Watch observed, "Under international law, governments have an obligation to provide effective remedies for violations of human rights." But will they—and we—comply? Will we ensure, through our actions, that the Tulsa Race Massacre of 1921 will happen *Never Again*?

ACKNOWLEDGMENTS

First and foremost, this book would not have been written without the encouragement and guidance of Dr. Sue A. Greer and Dr. Virginia Dodge Fielder. Jenny, one of my dearest friends, worked countless hours editing and shaping my raw manuscript into the book it is. I could not have done it without her and Sue.

After that, dozens of colleagues, friends, family, and strangers aided and abetted this arduous and exciting process. I am especially indebted to the group of extraordinary individuals who graciously agreed to read my final manuscript prior to publication: Pat Atkinson, longtime newspaper journalist and former associate managing editor of the *Tulsa World*; Connie Cronley, Tulsa author and citizen of the Cherokee Nation; Kim Hoover, attorney, author, and current president of the Lambda Literary board of trustees; Apple Gidley, Anglo-Australian author living in and writing about St. Croix; Dr. Kimberly R. Mills, senior executive director of the Center for Excellence in Developmental Disabilities at the University of the Virgin Islands; Annise Parker, former mayor of Houston, Texas, and current CEO of the Victory Fund and Rev. Dr. Robert Turner, pastor of Vernon Chapel AME Church in Tulsa.

Other readers and editors entered the picture at various times: my sister Patricia Atkins, Diane Butler, Angela Lake, Abigail Perry, Senufa Salley, and Fran Weinstein. I also wish to thank Ian Backer and Karlee Dies at Fulton Books for guiding me through the world of publishing.

Invaluable assistance has been generously offered by so many Tulsans, including Michelle Brown of the Greenwood Cultural Center; Roberta Clardy, owner of *NORTH TULSA* magazine; Tom

Gilbert and Tim Stanley, both of the *Tulsa World*; Rebecca Marks Jimerson, multicultural diversity trainer for Tulsa Community College Northeast Campus; Arlene Johnson, president of Arlene Johnson & Associates PR in Tulsa; and Martin Newman, Tulsa realtor and incorporator of Cottages at Maple Ridge Homeowners Association. Mallory Covington of the Oklahoma Historical Society and Luke Williams of the Tulsa Historical Society & Museum provided images for the book.

I would be remiss if I did not acknowledge my particular indebtedness to authors Scott Ellsworth, Eddie Faye Gates, James S. Hirsch, Bob Hower, Hannibal Johnson, Randy Krehbiel, and Tim Madigan. I relied heavily on their well-written, well-researched books to ensure the accuracy of the nonfictional events of this story. These books are listed in the bibliography compiled by Sara Daly.

Finally, my deepest gratitude goes to Crystal Weathers, my wife and the love of my life, who encouraged me every step of the way. She helped me conduct research, provided IT support, and kept the household running while I was otherwise occupied. I'd be lost without her.

APPENDIX 1

Map of Indian and Oklahoma Territories 1892

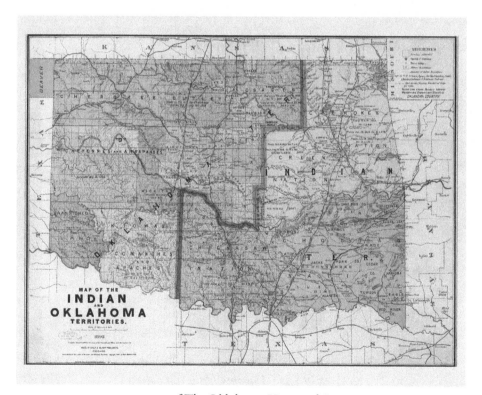

courtesy of The Oklahoma Historical Society

APPENDIX 2

Map of All-Black Towns of Oklahoma 1880–2020

All-Black Towns of Oklahoma
Oklahoma Historical Society | www.okhistory.org

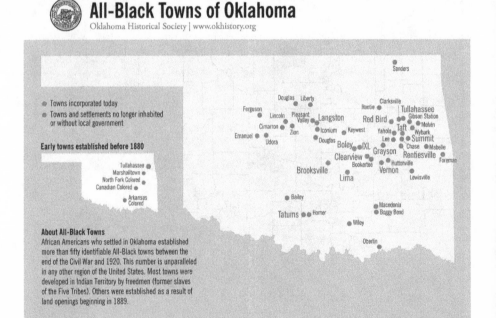

courtesy of The Oklahoma Historical Society

APPENDIX 3

Map of Greenwood District 2021

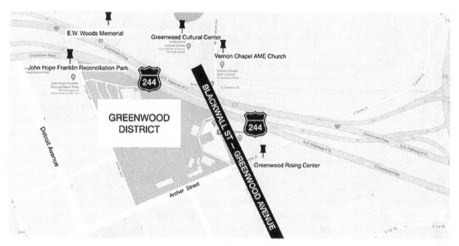

by Crystal Weathers

APPENDIX 4

Annotated Map of Tulsa Race Massacre of 1921

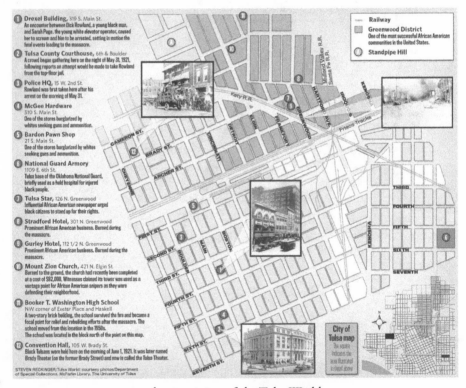

by permission of the Tulsa World

BIBLIOGRAPHY

Archival Sources and Collections

"Address by Mayor T. D. Evans to the city of Tulsa's Commissioners Board, June 14, 1921. African American Resource Center, Tulsa, Oklahoma.

Books

Dray, Philip. *At the Hands of Persons Unknown: The Lynching of Black America.* New York: Random House Publishing Group, 2002.

Ellsworth, Scott. *Death in a Promised Land: The Tulsa Race Riot of 1921.* Baton Rouge, Louisiana: Louisiana State University Press, 1982.

Gates, Eddie Faye. *Riot on Greenwood: The Total Destruction of Black Wall Street.* Austin, Texas: Sunbelt Eakin Press, 2003.

Greenbaum, Susan D. *The Afro-American Community in Kansas City, Kansas: A History.* Kansas City, Kansas: The City, 1982.

Greenwood Cultural Center. *Greenwood Cultural Center: Jewel in the Crown.* Virginia Beach, Virginia: The Donning Company Publishers, 2008.

Hirsch, James S. *Riot and Remembrance: The Tulsa Race War and Its Legacy.* New York: Houghton Mifflin Company, 2002.

Hower, Bob. *1921 Tulsa Race Riot: "America's Deadliest."* Tulsa, Oklahoma: Homestead Press, 1993.

Johnson, Hannibal B. *Acres of Aspiration: The All Black Towns in Oklahoma.* Austin, Texas: Eakin Press, 2002.

———. *Black Wall Street: From Riot to Renaissance in Tulsa's Historic Greenwood District.* Austin, Texas: Eakin Press, 1998.

———. *Black Wall Street 100: An American City Grapples with Its Historical Racial Trauma.* Austin, Texas: Eakin Press, 2020.

Krehbiel, Randy. *Tulsa 1921: Reporting a Massacre.* Norman, Oklahoma: University of Oklahoma Press, 2019.

Madigan, Tim. *The Burning: Massacre, Destruction, and the Tulsa Race Riot of 1921.* New York: Thomas Dunne Books, St. Martin's Press, 2001.

Maxine Horner, "Epilogue 1921," NORTH TULSA, https://www.northtulsa.org/index.php/images-of-1921/maxine-horner-epilogue. Accessed February 16, 2021.

Parrish, Mary E. Jones. *Race Riot 1921: Events of the Tulsa Disaster.* Tulsa, Oklahoma. Out on a Limb Publishing, 1998.

Ross, Don. "A Century of African-American Experience: Greenwood, Ruins, Resilience and Renaissance." A study guide based on an unpublished manuscript, *Pride and Infamy—The Black Wall Street of America.* Greenwood Cultural Center, Tulsa, Oklahoma, 2003.

The Race Reader—A Literary Chronicle of Conflict and Oppression in the Middle of America. Tulsa, Oklahoma: This Land Press, 2017.

Newspapers and Magazines Dated 1921

"85 Whites and Negroes Die in Tulsa Riot as 3,000 Armed Men Battle in Streets, 30 Blocks Burned, Military Rule in City." *New York Times*, June 2, 1921.

"Black Agitators Blamed for Riot." *Tulsa World*, June 6, 1921.

"Grand Jury Blames Negroes for Inciting Race Rioting: Whites Clearly Exonerated." *Tulsa World*, June 26, 1921, pp. 1, 8.

"Harding Denounces Fatal Tulsa Riots." *Washington Post*, June 7, 1921, p. 1.

"It Must Not Be Again." *Tulsa Tribune*, June 4, 1921.

"Jury Summons Being Issued for Riot Quiz." *Tulsa Tribune*, June 4, 1921.

"Lesson of Tulsa." *Chicago Daily Tribune*, June 3, 1921, p. 8.

"Loot, Arson, Murder! Four Million Dollars Lost, Sarah Page Not to Be Found, Tulsa Yanks Land Away from Blacks with Fire Ordinance." *Black Dispatch*, June 10, 1921.

"Nab Negro for Attacking Girl in Elevator." *Tulsa Tribune*, May 31, 1921.

"To Lynch Negro Tonight." *Tulsa Tribune*, May 31, 1921.

"Tulsa Race Riot: Jury Indicts Police Chief." *New York Times*, June 26, 1921, p. 16.

"Tulsa Race Riot Will Be Probed." *Atlanta Constitution*, June 3, 1921.

Commander, Tulsa Post African Blood Brotherhood. "The Tulsa Riot." *Crusader*, July 1921, pp. 5–25.

White, Walter F. "The Eruption of Tulsa." *Nation*, June 29, 1921, pp. 909–910.

Taft, William Howard. "Taft Charges Riots at Tulsa Was Due Largely to Whites." *Washington Post*, June 6, 1921.

Newspapers and Magazines After 1921

"Editorial Writers Consider Race Riot Panel." *Daily Oklahoman*, Feb. 1, 2000.

"Just 30 Years Ago Column." *Tulsa World*, June 1, 1951, p. 20.

"Just 30 Years Ago Column." *Tulsa World*, June 2, 1951, p. 4.

"Just 30 Years Ago Column." *Tulsa World*, June 4, 1951, p. 6.

"Just 30 Years Ago Column." *Tulsa World*, June 1, 1951, p. 20.

"Just 30 Years Ago Column." *Tulsa World*, June 2, 1951, p. 4.

"Just 30 Years Ago Column." *Tulsa World*, June 4, 1951, p. 6.

"Murderous Race Riot Wrote Red Page in Tulsa History 50 Years Ago." *Tulsa Tribune*, June 2, 1971, p. 7A.

"North Tulsans Need to Lead Memorials of the Tulsa Race Massacre." *Tulsa World*, May 26, 2019. http://www.tulsa-world.com/opinion/editorials/tulsa-world-editorial-north-tul-

sans-need-to-lead-memorials-of-tulsa-race-massacre/article_
c2e47b6f-dbc8-5d2d-8b84-a5021cfde4ca.html.

"Oklahoma Clears Black in Deadly 1921 Race Riot." *New York Times*,
October 26, 1996. http://www.nytimes.com/1996/10/26/
us/oklahoma-clears-black-in-deadly-1921-race-riot.html?
searchResultPosition=1.

"OSU-Tulsa Plans Memorial of Historic School Site." *Daily
O'Collegian*, Oklahoma State University, March 24, 2000.
http://www.ocolly.com/osu-tulsa-plans-memorial-of-histor-
ical-school-site/article_fb12aaea-30cd-5b0b-a56e-f23ce177
e0f1.html/.

"Panel Wraps Up Inquiry into Tulsa Race Riot." *Kansas City Star*,
February 23, 2001.

"Report Reveals Facts of 1921 Race Riot against Blacks in Oklahoma."
Militant, March 26, 2001.

"Tulsa Race Riot Panel Recommends Reparations." *Philadelphia
Inquirer*, February 5, 2000.

Briscoe, Darren. "Day of Reckoning." *Newsweek*, March 10, 2005.

Brown, Wesley. "Up from the Ashes… Greenwood District Rises
Above Rioting, Racism, Urban Renewal." *Tulsa World*, March
8, 1993, p. A9.

Brune, Adrian. "A Long Wait for Justice." *Village
Voice*, April 29, 2003. http://www.villagevoice.
com/2003/04/29/a-long-wait-for-justice/.

———. "Tulsa's Shame." *Nation*, March 18, 2002. http://www.
thenation.com/article/archive/tulsas-shame/.

Cheney-Rice, Zak. "Oklahoma Will Require Its Schools to Teach the
Tulsa Race Massacre of 1921." *New York Magazine*, February
21, 2020. http://www.nymag.com/intelligencer/2020/02/
oklahoma-schools-to-teach-1921-tulsa-massacre/.

Cremin, Pat. "Greenwood Is Fading." *Oklahoma Impact Magazine* 4,
June/July 1971, pp. 3–5.

Cronley, Connie. "That Ugly Day in May." *Oklahoma Monthly*,
August 1976.

Denniston, Lyle. "Judge Dismisses Riots Reparations Suit: While
Lamenting Tulsa Atrocity, He Cites Late Deadline." *Boston Globe*,

March 23, 2004. http://archive.boston.com/news/nation/articles/2004/03/23/judge_dismisses_riots_reparations_suit/.

Earley, Pete. "The Untold Story of One of America's Worst Race Riots." *Washington Post*, September 12, 1982. http://www.washingtonpost.com/archive/opinions/1982/09/12/the-untold-story-of-one-of-americas-worst-race-riots/e37fc963-71dd-45cc-8cb0-04ab8032bcd2/.

Gerkin, Steve. "BENO Hall Tulsa's Den of Terror." *This Land Magazine* 2, no. 11 (September 1, 2011).

Graham, Bob. "Why Has the Truth Behind the 1921 Race Riot of Tulsa, Oklahoma, Taken Nearly 80 Years to Emerge?" *Sunday Times Magazine*, May 20, 2001.

Holden, Mary Wisniewski. "75 Years Later: Vindication in Tulsa." *Chicago Lawyer*, December 1996.

Jones, Chris. "Dust Bowl Defined Worst of Times." *Oklahoman*, April 24, 1994. http://www.oklahoman.com/article/2464074/dust-bowl-defined-worst-of-times.

Kolker, Claudia. "A City's Buried Shame—Tulsa's Long Cover-Up of Horrific 1921 Race Riot Prompts a Search for a Mass Grave." *Los Angeles Times*, October 23, 1999.

Krehbiel, Randy. "Big-Name Attorneys Join Riot Lawsuit." *Tulsa World*, February 26, 2003. http://www.tulsaworld.com/archive/big-name-attorneys-join-riot-lawsuit/article_a46f9293-febb-50db-8569-d1903ace16c8/.

Krugman, Paul. "Tulsa and the Many Sins of Racism." *New York Times*, June 18, 2020. http://www.nytimes.com/2020/06/18/opinion/tulsa-race-massacre-racism.html.

Neal, Ken. "The Racial Puzzle." *Tulsa World*, June 9, 1996. http://www.tulsaworld.com/archive/the-racial-puzzle/article_e1c064fc-fa60-532b-ba47-7fff274ed666.html.

Patrick, James. "The Tulsa Race Riot of 1921: Part Two." *Exodus News*, October 12, 2005.

Staples, Brent. "The Burning of Black Wall Street, Revisited." *New York Times*, June 19, 2020. http://www.nytimes.com/2020/06/19/opinion/tulsa-race-riot-massacre-graves.html?searchResultPosition=1.

———. "Coming to Grips with the Unthinkable in Tulsa: Restitution for the Government's Role in Killing a Community." *New York Times*, March 16, 2003, p. 12.

———. "Unearthing a Riot." *New York Times*, December 19, 1999. http://www.nytimes.com/1999/12/19/magazine/unearthing-a-riot.html?searchResultPosition=1.

Sulzberger, A. G. "As Survivors Dwindle, Tulsa Confronts Past." *New York Times*, June 19, 2011. http://www.nytimes.com/2011/06/20/us/20tulsa.html?searchResultPosition=1.

Wheeler, Ed. "Profile of a Race Riot." *Oklahoma Impact Magazine* 4 (June/July 1971): 14–26.

Yardley, Jim. "Panel Recommends Reparations in Long-Ignored Tulsa Race Riot." *New York Times*, February 5, 2000. https://www.nytimes.com/2000/02/05/us/panel-recommends-reparations-in-long-ignored-tulsa-race-riot.html?searchResultPosition=1.

Other Sources

"For Now, No Reparations for Tulsa Race Riot Victims," *SeeingBlack.com*, June 21, 2001.

"Oklahoma City Bombing," *History.com*, May 20, 2020. http://www.history.com/topics/1990s/oklahoma-city-bombing.

"Tulsa No Longer Silent About Catastrophic Race Riot—Documentary Explores Causes and Effects of 1921 Massacre," *APBnews.com*, May 31, 2000.

"Tulsa Panel Seeks Truth from 1921 Race Riot," *CNN*, Aug. 3, 1999.

"Unearthing Ugly History," *ABC News*, Nov. 11, 1999.

Ackerman, Lauren. "Bricktown and Deep Deuce, Oklahoma City (1889–)." Blackpast.org, March 19, 2016. http://www.blackpast.org/african-american-history/bricktown-and-deep-deuce-oklahoma-city-1889/.

Brophy, Alfred L. "Who Pays: In Oklahoma, Another Debate about Reparations." Tomepaine.com, July 27, 2000.

Carlson, I. Marc. *The Tulsa Race Riot of 1921—Some Questions about the Race Riot of 1921*. University of Tulsa, 2000. http://www.personal.utulsa.edu/~marc-carlson/riot/riotques.html.

Cooper, Kelly-Leigh. "Oklahoma City Bombing: The Day Domestic Terror Shook America." BBC News, April 18, 2020. http://www.bbc.com/news/world-us-canada-51735115.

Greenlaw, Marshall. "Indian Severalty (the Dawes and Curtis Acts) and Black Indian Freedmen." Blackpast.org, July 16, 2017. http://www.blackpast.org/african-american-history/indian-severalty-dawes-and-curtis-acts-and-black-indian-freedmen/.

Halliburton, R. Jr. "The Tulsa Race War of 1921." *Journal of Black Studies* 2, no. 3 (March 1972): 333–357.

Heath, Dreisen. "The Case for Reparations in Tulsa, Oklahoma." Human Rights Watch, May 29, 2020. http://www.hrw.org/news/2020/05/29/case-reparations-tulsa-oklahoma.

Maita, Joe. "Tulsa in 1921—an Interview with Tim Madigan, Author of The Burning: Massacre, Destruction, and the Tulsa Race Riot of 1921." Jerryjazzmusician.com, April 12, 2002. http://www.jerryjazzmusician.com/2002/04/tim-madigan-author-of-the-burning-massacre-destruction-and-the-tulsa-race-riot-of-1921/.

Maxouris, Christina. "1921 Tulsa Race Massacre Will Soon Be a Part of the Curriculum for Oklahoma Schools." CNN.com, February 20, 2020. http://www.cnn.com/2020/02/20/us/oklahoma-schools-1921-race-massacre-trnd/index.html.

Moreno, Carlos. "Examining Tulsa's Greater Sin: From the Massacre through Today." Beyond Belief. http://www.beyondbelief.online/examining-tulsa/. Accessed January 9, 2021.

Savage, Charles. "Survivors of 1921 Tulsa Riot Petition Supreme Court for Reparations." *Boston Globe*, March 10, 2005, accessed January 9, 2021 via *Brownwatch*. http://www.brown-watch.com/to-the-present/2005/3/11/survivors-of-1921-tulsa-race-riot-petition-supreme-court-for-reparations.html?rq=tulsa%201921.

Wilkerson, Michael, dir. *Tulsa Lynching of 1921: A Hidden Story*. Barrister Studios, 2000.

ABOUT THE AUTHOR

Susan E. Atkins is a retired media relations professional with more than forty years of communications experience, including teaching journalism at the University of Tulsa. A former vice president of a Fortune 500 company, she founded her own media relations company and later sold it to an international firm.

An Oklahoma native, she grew up in Tulsa and earned bachelor's and master's degrees from the University of Oklahoma. She also earned an MBA from Pepperdine University in California, where she lived for forty years. Susan now resides in the US Virgin Islands with her wife, Crystal Weathers, cat, Golden Boy, and two Crucian rescue dogs, Sassy and Snoop Doggie Dog

She is currently on the board of the Caribbean Museum Center for the Arts and has served on the board of the Women's Coalition of St. Croix. Other volunteer positions include serving as vice president of the board of trustees of Lambda Literary, chair of the board of the Victory Fund, member of the board of Equally American, and library commissioner in San Diego, California.

CPSIA information can be obtained
at www.ICGtesting.com
Printed in the USA
LVHW051545280422
716896LV00001B/6